James Hadley Chase and The Murder Room

>>> This title is part of The Murder Room, our series dedicated to making available out-of-print or hard-to-find titles by classic crime writers.

Crime fiction has always held up a mirror to society. The Victorians were fascinated by sensational murder and the emerging science of detection; now we are obsessed with the forensic detail of violent death. And no other genre has so captivated and enthralled readers.

Vast troves of classic crime writing have for a long time been unavailable to all but the most dedicated frequenters of second-hand bookshops. The advent of digital publishing means that we are now able to bring you the backlists of a huge range of titles by classic and contemporary crime writers, some of which have been out of print for decades.

From the genteel amateur private eyes of the Golden Age and the femmes fatales of pulp fiction, to the morally ambiguous hard-boiled detectives of mid twentieth-century America and their descendants who walk our twenty-first century streets, The Murder Room has it all. >>>

The Murder Room
Where Criminal Minds Meet

themurderroom.com

T0352485

James Hadley Chase (1906–1985)

Born René Brabazon Raymond in London, the son of a British colonel in the Indian Army, James Hadley Chase was educated at King's School in Rochester, Kent, and left home at the age of 18. He initially worked in book sales until, inspired by the rise of gangster culture during the Depression and by reading James M. Cain's *The Postman Always Rings Twice*, he wrote his first novel, *No Orchids for Miss Blandish*. Despite the American setting of many of his novels, Chase (like Peter Cheyney, another hugely successful British noir writer) never lived there, writing with the aid of maps and a slang dictionary. He had phenomenal success with the novel, which continued unabated throughout his entire career, spanning 45 years and nearly 90 novels. His work was published in dozens of languages and over thirty titles were adapted for film. He served in the RAF during World War II, where he also edited the RAF Journal. In 1956 he moved to France with his wife and son; they later moved to Switzerland, where Chase lived until his death in 1985.

By James Hadley Chase
(published in The Murder Room)

No Orchids for Miss Blandish
Eve
More Deadly Than the Male
Mission to Venice
Mission to Siena
Not Safe to Be Free
Shock Treatment
Come Easy – Go Easy
What's Better Than Money?
Just Another Sucker
I Would Rather Stay Poor
A Coffin from Hong Kong
Tell it to the Birds
One Bright Summer Morning
The Soft Centre
You Have Yourself a Deal
Have This One on Me
Well Now, My Pretty
Believed Violent
An Ear to the Ground
The Whiff of Money
The Vulture Is a Patient Bird
Like a Hole in the Head
An Ace Up My Sleeve

Want to Stay Alive?
Just a Matter of Time
You're Dead Without Money
Have a Change of Scene
Knock, Knock! Who's There?
Goldfish Have No Hiding Place
So What Happens to Me?
The Joker in the Pack
Believe This, You'll Believe
    Anything
Do Me a Favour – Drop Dead
I Hold the Four Aces
My Laugh Comes Last
Consider Yourself Dead
You Must Be Kidding
A Can of Worms
Try This One for Size
You Can Say That Again
Hand Me a Fig-Leaf
Have a Nice Night
We'll Share a Double Funeral
Not My Thing
Hit Them Where It Hurts

Do Me a Favour – Drop Dead

James Hadley Chase

An Orion book

Copyright © Hervey Raymond 1976

The right of James Hadley Chase to be identified as the author of this work has been asserted in accordance with the Copyright, Designs and Patents Act 1988.

This edition published by
The Orion Publishing Group Ltd
Orion House
5 Upper St Martin's Lane
London WC2H 9EA

An Hachette UK company
A CIP catalogue record for this book is available from the British Library

ISBN 978 1 4719 0392 2

www.orionbooks.co.uk

HE JOINED the Greyhound at Sacramento and settled his bulk on the outside seat, next to mine.

He looked as if he had stepped straight out of the 19th century with his Mark Twain moustache, his string tie, his grey alpaca suit and his white Stetson. He was around sixty-five years of age and had a belly on him that could have been mistaken in the dark for a garbage can. He wore his hair long, Buffalo Bill style, and his red face signalled an inner contentment and a bonhomie that are rare these days.

Once he had settled himself, taken a quick look around, he turned his attention to me. As the bus was moving off, he said, " Howdy. I'm Joe Pinner of Wicksteed."

I was aware that his small brown eyes were taking in my shabby suit that had cost two hundred dollars six years ago and was past its best. The small brown eyes also took in the frayed cuffs of my shirt that was showing grime after the long stint in this bus.

I said curtly, " Keith Devery of New York."

He puffed out his fat cheeks, took off his Stetson, wiped his forehead, put on the Stetson, then said in a mild voice, " New York? You've come a long way. Me . . . I've seen New York : not my neck of the woods."

" Not mine either."

The bus jolted us together. His shoulder hit mine. His was all muscle and hard fat. Mine took the shock.

" You know Wicksteed, Mr. Devery?" he asked.

" No." I wasn't interested. I wanted quiet, but I could see I wasn't going to get it.

" Finest little town on the Pacific coast," he told me. " Only fifty miles from 'Frisco. Has the finest little hospital, the most prosperous commercial trading, the best self-service store between L.A. and 'Frisco, even though I say it who owns it." He gave a rumbling laugh. " You should stop off, Mr. Devery and take a look."

" I'm heading for 'Frisco."

" Is that right? I know 'Frisco : not my neck of the woods." He took out a well worn cigar case and offered it. I shook my head. " For a young, energetic man, Wicksteed offers opportunities." He lit the cigar, puffed rich smelling smoke, then relaxed back in his seat. " Would you be looking for a job, Mr. Devery?"

" Right." I thought back on the past ten months which had been a series of jobs and what jobs! I was now worth fifty-nine dollars and seven cents. Once that was spent, nothing remained. Yes, I was looking for a job . . . any job. I couldn't get lower than my last job : dish washing in a crummy wayside café . . . or couldn't I?

Pinner puffed at his cigar.

" You could do worse taking a look at Wicksteed," he said. " It's a friendly little town . . . it likes to help people."

That last remark made me sore.

" Do you think I need help?" I asked, a snap in my voice.

He removed his cigar, eyed it, before saying, " I guess everyone at some time in their lives can do with a little help."

" That's not what I asked." I half turned to glare at him.

" Well, Mr. Devery, I get the impression you could do with some friendly help," he said mildly, " but if I'm wrong, excuse me and forget it."

I turned away and stared out of the dusty window. Over my

shoulder, I growled, " I don't ask favours nor expect them."

He didn't say anything to this and I kept staring out of the window, and after a while I heard him snoring gently. I turned to look at him. He was asleep, his cigar held between two thick fingers, his Stetson pushed down over his eyes.

It is just on ninety miles from Sacramento to 'Frisco. I'd be lucky to get there in three and a half hours. I hadn't had any breakfast and I had a thirst on me that would have slain a camel. I had used up my last cigarette. I was now regretting I had refused his cigar.

I sat there, watching the scenery, feeling pretty low, wondering if I had made the right decision to leave the Atlantic seaboard for the Pacific seaboard. I reminded myself that I still had a few friends in and around New York, and although they couldn't help me get a job, if things got really rough, I could have screwed them for a loan. The Pacific seaboard was an unknown quantity and no friends to screw.

After an hour or so, I saw a sign post that read : *Wicksteed. 40 miles.* Joe Pinner woke up, yawned, looked past me out of the window and grunted.

" Not long now," he said. " Do you drive a car, Mr. Devery ?"

" Why, sure."

" Would a driving instructor's job interest you ?"

I frowned at him.

" Driving instructor? You need qualifications for a job like that."

" Nothing to get excited about in Wicksteed. We are an easy going lot. You need to be a good driver, have a clean licence and tons of patience . . . that's about it. My old friend Bert Ryder needs a driving instructor. He owns the Wicksteed Driving-school and his man's in hospital. It makes it awkward for Bert. He's never touched a car in his life. He's strictly a horse an' buggy man." He relit his cigar, then went on, " That's what I meant about helping people, Mr. Devery. He could help you and you could help him. The job's nothing

3

big: it pays two hundred, but it's easy and keeps you out in the open air and two hundred is eating money, ain't it?"

"That's right, but maybe he's found someone by now." I tried to conceal my eagerness.

"He hadn't this morning."

"I could ask him."

"You do that." Pinner hoisted a hold-all that had been resting between his feet onto his knees. He zipped it open and took out a parcel made up with grease proof paper. "My old lady imagines, when I go on a trip, I might forget to eat." He gave his rumbling laugh. "Will you join me in a sandwich, Mr. Devery?"

For a moment I was going to refuse, then seeing the white fresh bread, the chicken breasts and sliced gerkins, I said, "Why thanks, Mr. Pinner."

"The truth is I had lunch before I got on the bus. It's more than my life's worth to take this lot back uneaten. You go ahead, Mr. Devery," and he dumped the parcel on my lap.

I went ahead. My last meal had been a greasy hamburger last night. By the time I had eaten the four sandwiches, we were approaching Wicksteed. It certainly looked a nice town. The main street ran along the Pacific ocean. There were palm trees and flowering oleander shrubs. The people on the side-walks looked prosperous. On a distant corner was a big super-market with *Pinner's Super Bazaar* in neon lights on the roof.

The bus came to a halt.

"That's my place," Pinner said, heaving himself out of his seat. "You'll find Bert Ryder's school a block further on. Tell him you are a friend of mine, Mr. Devery."

We got out of the bus with five or six other people.

"Thanks, Mr. Pinner," I said. "I appreciate this, and thanks for the sandwiches."

"You were helping me to get rid of them." He laughed. "There's a men's room in the bus station if you want to spruce up. Good luck." He shook hands and walked off towards the store.

Lugging my shabby suitcase, I went to the men's room, had a wash and a shave and put on my one clean shirt. I stared at myself in the mirror. You don't spend five years in a tough jail without it showing. My black hair had white streaks in it. My face was gaunt with a night-club pallor. Although I had been out now for ten months, I still had that jail-bird look.

I spent a dime on a shoe-shine machine, then deciding there was nothing else I could do to make myself more presentable, I set off in search of Ryder's Driving school. I found it as Pinner had said on the next block : a one-storey building, painted a gay yellow and white with a big sign on the roof. The door stood open and I walked in.

A girl who looked as if she was just out of school, her hair in pig tails, her round, bright face pretty in the way kids can look before they discover how tough the world really is, stopped her typing and smiled.

" Mr. Ryder in ? "

" In there." She pointed. " Go ahead. He isn't busy."

I put down my suitcase.

" Okay for me to leave this here ? "

" I'll watch it." She smiled.

I tapped on the door, opened it and entered a small office. Seated at a desk was a man who reminded me a little of Harry S. Truman. He would be around seventy-five years of age, balding with spectacles. He got to his feet with a wide, friendly smile.

" Come on in," he said. " I'm Bert Ryder."

" Keith Devery."

" Take a pew. What can I do for you, Mr. Devery ? "

I sat down and squeezed my hands between my knees

" I ran into Joe Pinner on the bus," I said. " He thought I could help you and you could help me. I understand you're looking for a driving instructor, Mr. Ryder."

He took out a pack of Camels, shook out two cigarettes, rolled one across the desk towards me and lit his, then he passed the lighter to me. While he was doing this, his grey eyes surveyed me quizzingly. That was okay by me. I was used to prospective employers surveying me. I looked straight back at him as I lit the cigarette.

" Joe Pinner, huh?" He nodded. " A great guy for thinking of others. Have you any experience as a driving instructor, Mr. Devery?"

" No, but I am a good driver. I have a clean licence and I have a ton of patience. According to Mr. Pinner those are the only necessary qualifications."

Ryder chuckled.

" That's about correct." He reached out a brown, heavily veined hand. " May I see your licence?"

I dug it out of my billfold and gave it to him.

He studied it for a few moments.

" New York? You're a long way from home."

" New York isn't my home. I just happened to work there."

" I see you stopped driving for five years, Mr. Devery."

" That's right. I couldn't afford to run a car any more."

He nodded.

" You're thirty-eight: a fine age. I'd like to be thirty-eight again." He pushed the licence back to me. " What car did you drive, Mr. Devery?"

" A Thunderbird."

" A nice car." He flicked ash into the glass ash tray. " You know, Mr. Devery, I think you could be wasting your talents by taking this job. I like to imagine I'm a good judge of men. What have you been doing with yourself all these years if I may ask?"

" Oh, this and that." I shrugged. " Call me footloose, Mr. Ryder. I was washing dishes the night before last. A week ago, I was cleaning cars."

Again he nodded.

" Would it be impertinent to ask why you received a five-year stretch?"

I stared at him, then shrugged. I pushed back my chair and stood up.

" I'm sorry to have taken up your time, Mr. Ryder," I said. " I didn't think it showed so plainly," and I started towards the door.

" Don't run away," Ryder said quietly. " It doesn't show all that plainly but my son got out a couple of years ago and I remember how he looked when he came home. He went inside for eight years : armed robbery."

I paused, my hand on the door knob and stared at him. His face was impassive as he waved me back to the chair.

" Sit down, Mr. Devery. I tried to help him, but he wouldn't be helped. I believe in helping people who have tripped up, so long as they are frank with me."

I returned to the chair and sat down.

" What happened to your son, Mr. Ryder?"

" He's dead. He hadn't been out more than three months before he tried to rob a bank He killed the bank guard and the police killed him." Ryder frowned at his cigarette. " Well, that's the way things can happen. I blame myself. I didn't try hard enough. There are always two sides to a story. I didn't listen hard enough to his."

" Maybe it wouldn't have made any difference."

" Maybe . . ." His smile was sad. " Do you want to tell me your story, Mr. Devery?"

" Only on the condition that you don't have to believe it."

" No one has to believe anything he's told, but there is no harm in listening." He stubbed out his cigarette. " Would you do me a favour, Mr. Devery? Would you turn the key in the lock?"

Surprised, I got to my feet and locked the door. As I returned to my chair, I saw a bottle of Johnny Walker and two shot glasses had materialised.

" Wouldn't like Maisie to come in and find us men drinking," he said and winked. " I like kids to respect their elders."

With loving care, he poured two shots, pushed one glass towards me and lifted the other.

" Here's to the young and innocent."

We drank.

" Now, Mr. Devery, you were going to tell me . . ."

" I was what is called a broker's front man," I said. " I worked for Barton Sharman, the second biggest brokerage house after Merrill Lynch. I was regarded as a whizz-kid. I was ambitious. I got drafted to Vietnam. They held my job open, but it wasn't the same when I got back. In Vietnam I met ambitious guys and they taught me how to make a very fast buck in the black market. Making money for other people wasn't fun any more. I wanted to make money for myself. A very secret merger came up. I got a whisper of it. It was a chance of a life-time. I used a client's money. With my know-how, it was easy. I stood to make three quarters of a million. There was a last minute foul-up. The lid blew off and I drew five years. That's it. No one got hurt except me. I asked for it and I got it. I'm only good with figures and no one is going to give me a job where there's cash around so I take what I can find."

He refilled our glasses.

" Are you still ambitious, Mr. Devery?"

" There's no point in being ambitious if you can't deal with figures," I said. " No . . . five years in a cell have taught me to lower my sights."

" Are your parents alive?"

" Long dead . . . killed in an air crash before I went to Vietnam. I'm strictly on my own."

" Married?"

" I was, but she didn't want to wait five years."

He finished his drink, then nodded.

" You can have the job. It pays two hundred. It's not much for someone like you who has been used to better things, but I don't expect you to make a career of it. Let's say it's a marking time job to better things."

" Thanks . . . what do I have to do?"

" Teach people to drive. Mostly they are kids . . . nice kids, but every now and then we get middle-aged people . . . nice people. You work from nine to six. We are pretty booked up as Tom is in hospital. Tom Lucas . . . my instructor. He had bad luck . . . got an elderly woman who drove into a truck. She was all right, but Tom got concussion. You have to be alert, Mr. Devery. There are no dual controls, but you share the handbrake. Just keep your fingers on the handbrake and you'll be fine."

I finished my drink. He finished his, then put the bottle and the glasses back in his desk.

" When do I start?"

" Tomorrow morning. Talk to Maisie. She'll tell you your appointments. Treat Maisie nice, Mr. Devery. She's a real nice kid."

He took out his billfold and put a hundred dollar bill on the desk.

" Maybe you could use an advance. Then you want somewhere to live. Let me recommend Mrs. Hansen. I expect Joe Pinner told you this is a great little town for helping people. Mrs. Hansen has just lost her husband. She is a mite hard up. She owns a nice house on Seaview avenue. She has decided to let a room. She'll make you comfortable. She charges thirty a week and that includes breakfast and dinner. I've seen the room . . . it's nice."

It seemed ' nice ' was the operative word in Wicksteed.

" I'll go along and see her." I paused, then went on, " And thank you for the job."

" You're helping me out, Keith." He raised his eyebrows. " You said your name was Keith?"

" That's right, Mr. Ryder."

" I'm Bert to everyone in town."

" Then I'll see you tomorrow, Bert," I said and went out to talk to Maisie.

*　　　*　　　*

I woke the following morning at 7.00.

9

For the first time in months, I had slept through the night without waking. This was a record for me.

I stretched, yawned and reached for a cigarette. I looked around the big, airy room.

Bert had called it nice. To me, living rough for the past ten months, this was an understatement.

It had a divan bed on which I was lying, two comfortable armchairs, a small dining table with two chairs, a colour TV set and by the big picture window a small desk and chair. Facing me was a wall to wall bookcase, crammed with books. There were two wool rugs, one by the divan, the other under the desk. The flooring was polished wood blocks. There was a small, vine-covered veranda that looked out onto the beach and the sea. For thirty bucks a week the room was a steal.

Before calling on Mrs. Hansen, I had gone to Pinner's Super Bazaar and had bought myself a couple of short sleeved shirts, two pairs of cotton slacks and a pair of sandals. Everyone in Wicksteed seemed to be in vacation gear.

Mrs. Hansen was a dumpy little woman of around fifty-eight. Her straw-coloured hair and her pale blue eyes were all Danish and she spoke with a slight guttural accent. She said Bert had telephoned about me. I wondered if he had warned her I was an ex-jailbird. I thought not. She took me into a big lounge with French windows looking onto the beach. The room was full of books. She explained that her husband had been the headmaster of the Wicksteed school. He had worked too hard and had had a fatal heart attack. I murmured the correct things. She said he had always been generous and had given away most of his money helping people. She said this with satisfaction. It was the right thing to do, she declared, but then he hadn't known he was going to pass on so soon. She had been left without much money. I would be her first lodger.

She took me upstairs and showed me the room. She explained it had been her husband's study. She said he had liked television, but she didn't, so if I wanted it, she would leave the set where it was. I thanked her. A little anxiously, she asked if thirty dollars would be all right. I said it would. She told me there were two bathrooms and mine was down the corridor. She lived downstairs. She said dinner would be at seven, but I could have it later if I wished. I said seven would be fine. She asked if I had any dislikes. Remembering what I had been eating lately I nearly laughed. I said I wasn't fussy. She said she would bring the meals up on a tray and would I like her to get some beer in which she would keep in the refrigerator. I said that would be fine. She hoped I would enjoy my work with Bert who (I waited for it) was a nice man. She said she had a black lady (probably nice too, I thought) who did the cleaning and would do my laundry. Would breakfast be all right at eight o'clock?

When she had gone, I unpacked, looked at some of the books but found they were strictly scholastic and there was no light reading. I went along to the bathroom and spent an hour soaking in hot water. Then I changed into my new outfit and went out onto the veranda. I watched the boys and the girls having fun on the beach until Mrs. Hansen brought up the dinner which consisted of fish pie, cheese and ice-cream. There was also a can of beer.

I took the tray down when I had finished and left it in the kitchen. Mrs. Hansen was out on the patio, reading. I didn't disturb her.

Back in my room, I sat on the veranda and smoked. I couldn't quite believe this was happening to me after those ten awful months when I had been living rough. Now, suddenly, I had a two hundred a week job and a real home. It was too good to be true. Later, I watched TV news, then went to bed. It was a nice bed. In the shaded light by the divan, I thought it was a nice room. I seemed to be catching the 'nice' habit. I went to sleep.

Lying on the divan, a cigarette between my fingers, I could hear Mrs. Hansen preparing my breakfast. I was going to have a busy day. Maisie (she had told me her name was Jean Maisie

Kent, but would I call her Maisie?) had shown me a list of pupils I was to teach. I had three one-hour lessons in the morning, an hour off for lunch, and five one hour lessons in the afternoon.

" They are all just out of school," she explained. " They are all beginners. The only one you have to be careful about is Hank Sobers. He is a show-off and thinks he knows it all. Just be careful of him, Mr. Devery."

I said I would and would she call me Keith as I was calling her Maisie?

She nodded. For her age (she couldn't have been more than sixteen) she was remarkably self-possessed. I asked about the Highway code, admitting I had forgotten most of it. She said not to worry as Bert took the code classes. That was a relief. All the same I borrowed a copy of the code from her, meaning to look at it that evening, but had forgotten to.

I shaved, took a shower and dressed, then went out onto the veranda. I thought about Bert Ryder. Up to a point I had been truthful when I had told him why I had been jailed for five years, but I hadn't been truthful about some of the details nor when he had asked if I was still ambitious. Ever since I had returned from Vietnam, after seeing the easy money made out of the black market, I had developed an itch for the big money. There was a Staff-sergeant who had been so well organised that, so he had told me, he and his three buddies would be worth close on a million dollars by the time they quit the Army. They had robbed the Army blind. They had even sold three Sherman tanks to a North Korean dealer to say nothing of cases of rifles, hand grenades, Army stores and so on. In the confusion of the fighting and during the Nixon pull-out, no one missed the tanks nor the stolen equipment. I had envied these men. A million dollars! Back at my desk at Barton Sharman I had kept thinking of that Staff-sergeant who looked more like an ape than a human being. So when this merger seemed about to jell, I didn't hesitate. This was my chance and I was going to take it! Once the merger went through, the share price would treble. I opened an account with a bank in Haverford and lodged with them Bearer bonds worth $450,000 which I was holding in safe keeping for a client of mine. With these bonds I bought the shares. When the merger went through, all I had to do was to sell, pick up the profit and return the bonds.

It looked good, but S.E.C. stepped in and the merger never was. I had lied to Bert when I had told him no one got hurt but me. My client lost his bonds, but I knew the bonds had been tax evasion money so he was almost, probably not quite, as big a thief as I was.

I had also lied to Bert when I had told him I was no longer ambitious. My ambition was like the spots of the leopard. Once you are landed with my kind of ambition, you were stuck with it. My ambition for big money burned inside me with the intensity of a blow-torch flame. It nagged me like raging toothache. During those five grim years in jail I had spent hours thinking and scheming about how to get my hands on big money. I kept telling myself what that ape-like Staff-sergeant could do, I could do. I hadn't lied to Bert when I had told him I had patience. I had that all right. Sooner or later, I was going to be rich. I was going to have a fine house, a Caddy, a yacht and all the other trimmings that big money buys. I was going to have all that. It would be tough, but I was going to have it. At the age of thirty-eight, starting now from scratch; and with a criminal record, it was going to be more than tough, but not, I told myself, impossible. I had rubbed shoulders enough in my Barton Sharman days with the tycoons, and I knew them to be what they were: tough, hard, ruthless and determined. Many of them were unethical and amoral. Their philosophy was: the weak to the wall; the strong takes the jack-pot.

My chance would come if I was patient, and when it did, nothing would stop me grabbing it. I would have to be tougher, harder, more ruthless, more determined, more unethical and more amoral than any of them.

If that was what I had to be, then that was what I was going to be!

Mrs. Hansen tapped on the door and brought in my breakfast. She asked if I had slept well and would I like fried chicken for dinner. I said that would be fine. When she had gone, I sat down to buckwheat pancakes and two eggs on grilled ham.

I told myself that when I got my first million, I would send Mrs. Hansen a big, anonymous donation. She was stealing herself blind.

*   *   *

" How did it go, Keith?" Bert asked as I came into his office for the lunch hour break. " Any problems?"

" No problems. These kids are certainly keen. It's my bet they have been practising on their father's cars. They can't be as good as this first time."

He chuckled.

" I guess that's right. Anyway, you like the work?"

" If you can call it work, I like it," I said. " I guess I'll go grab me a hamburger. See you at two."

" Oh, Keith, use the car. It's no use to me. I've never learned to drive, and I'm too old to start now. So long as you pay for the gas, it's yours."

" Why thanks, Bert."

" Mrs. Hansen has a garage at the back. It'll save you a bus fare."

" Nice idea." I underlined the word ' nice ' and grinned at him.

" You're catching on. Want a snort before you go?"

" Thanks, no. No hard stuff during working hours."

He nodded his approval.

I went over to the café across the street, ordered a hamburger and a Coke.

So far the job seemed dead easy. As I had told Bert, the kids were crazy to get their driving permits so they could take off in some old buggy they had saved for, and they were eager to learn. I seemed to have the knack of getting along with young people. I had mixed enough with them in Vietnam and I knew their thing. But, I told myself, I mustn't let myself get sucked into this easy way of life. It was fine for a month or so, but no longer. At the end of the month, unless some opportunity turned up—the big opportunity I was waiting for—then I would have to move on. I would take a look at 'Frisco. Surely in a City of that size the opportunity would be waiting.

When I returned to the Driving school a few minutes before two, I found Hank Sobers waiting. Remembering Maisie's warning, I looked him over. He was a tall, gangling youth of around eighteen with a crop of pimples, hair down to his shoulders, wearing a T-shirt on which was printed: *Don't Look Further Than Me, Babe.*

" This is Hank Sobers," Maisie said. " The boy wonder," and she went back to her typing.

" Hurry it up, dad," Hank said to me. " I ain't got all day."

I moved up and loomed over him. This had to be handled fast and right.

" Talking to me?" I barked.

They teach you how to bark in the Army, and I hadn't forgotten.

I startled him as I had meant to startle him. He took a step back and gaped at me.

" Let's get going," he said feebly. " I'm paying for these bloody lessons and I expect action."

I looked at Maisie who had stopped typing and was watching, her eyes round.

" Is he paying or is his father paying?"

" His father is."

" Right." I turned back to Hank. " Now listen, son, from now on you call me Mr. Devery . . . understand? When you get into that car, you will do exactly what I say. You won't voice your unwanted opinions. I'm going to teach you to drive. If you don't like the way I do it, go elsewhere. Get all that?"

I knew from what Maisie had told me there was no other

Driving school in Wicksteed so I had him where I wanted him.

He hesitated, then mumbled.

" Oh, sure."

" Oh sure . . . what?" Again the bark.

" Oh sure, Mr. Devery."

" Let's go." I took him out to the car. As soon as he got into the driving seat, started the engine and moved the car from the kerb, I could see he didn't need lessons. It was my bet he had been driving his old man's car without a permit for months. I told him to drive around, had him park, had him stop on a hill, had him U-turn. I couldn't fault him.

" Okay, pull up here."

He parked and looked at me.

" How's your driving code, Hank?"

" It's okay."

" Go talk to Mr. Ryder. If he passes you, I'll pass you. You don't need lessons. You handle a car as well as I do."

He suddenly grinned.

" Gee! Thanks, Mr. Devery. I thought you'd screw me around just to get my old man's money."

" That's an idea." I regarded him. " Maybe you'd better have five more lessons."

He looked alarmed.

" Hey! I was only kidding."

" So was I. Drive me back and I'll talk to Mr. Ryder."

We returned to the Driving school. I talked to Bert and he had Hank in and tested him.

Ten minutes later, Hank came out of Bert's office, a wide grin on his face.

" I walked it!" he said to me. " And thanks, Mr. Devery, you've been swell."

" You still have the official test to take," I reminded him. " So watch it."

" Sure will, Mr. Devery," and still grinning he took himself off.

" You certainly have a way with you, Keith," Maisie said.

She had been listening. "That voice! You scared me."

"An old Army trick," I said, but I was pleased with myself. "Who's next on the list?"

I knocked off just after 18.00, looked in to say so long to Bert, then getting in the car, I started down Main street towards my hired room.

A police whistle made me stiffen. I looked to my right. A tall man in brown uniform, a fawn Stetson on his head, a gun on his hip, crooked a finger at me.

My heart skipped a beat. For the past ten months I had steered clear of the cops. I had even got into the habit of crossing the street or stepping into a shop if I saw one coming. Well, there was no skipping this one. I checked my driving mirror, saw the street was clear of traffic behind me and pulled to the kerb.

I sat still, my hands moist, my heart thumping while I watched in my wing mirror his casual approach. Like all cops when stopping a car, he wasn't in a hurry—his way of waging a war of nerves—and finally, he came to rest beside me: a young guy, hatchet faced, small cop eyes, thin lips. The first non-nice person I had met in Wicksteed. He had a label on his shirt that read: Deputy sheriff Abel Ross.

"This your car, Mac?" he demanded, movie tough.

"No, and my name's not Mac, it's Devery."

He narrowed his narrow eyes.

"If it's not your car what are you doing driving it?"

"Going home, Deputy sheriff Ross," I said quietly, and I could see I was fazzing him a little.

"Mr. Ryder know about it, Mac?"

"The name's Devery, Deputy sheriff Ross," I said, "and he knows about it."

"Licence."

He held out a hand as big as a ham.

I gave him my licence and he studied it.

"You've renewed it. Why has it lapsed for five years?"

Now he was getting me fazzed.

17

" I gave up driving for five years."

" Why ?"

" I didn't need a car."

He cocked his head on one side, staring at me.

" Why didn't you need a car ?"

" For private reasons, Deputy sheriff Ross. Why do you ask ?"

After a long pause, he handed the licence back.

" I haven't seen you around before. What are you doing in this town ?"

" I am the new driving instructor," I told him. " If you want to check me out suppose you talk to Mr. Ryder ?"

" Yeah. We make a point of checking out strangers here. Especially guys who have given up driving for five years."

" What does that mean ?"

" You should know," he said, and turning, he stalked off down the sidewalk.

I sat for a long moment, staring through the windshield. I had served my sentence and there was nothing he could do about it, but I knew this could happen in any town I drove in. Once a jailbird to the cops, always a jailbird.

Across the way was a bar. Above the entrance was the simple legend : Joe's Bar. I felt in need of a drink. Locking the car, I crossed the street and went in.

The bar was big and dark and there were two fans in the ceiling churning up the hot air. For a moment or so, coming in from the bright sunlight, I couldn't see much, then my eyes adjusted to the dimness. Two men were propping up the long bar counter at the far end, talking to the barkeeper behind the counter. When he saw me, he walked the length of the counter to give me a broad smile of welcome.

" Howdy, Mr. Devery." At a guess, he was fiftyish, short, fat and happy looking. " Pleased to meet you. I'm Joe Summers. I own this joint . . . What's your pleasure ?"

" Scotch on the rocks, please." I regarded him, a little startled. " How did you know who I am ?"

He grinned.

"My boy had a driving lesson from you this morning, Mr. Devery. He tells me you're sharp. Coming from him who thinks anyone over twenty-five is square is praise."

"Sammy Summers?" I remembered the kid. He hadn't been one of the bright ones.

"That's him. Scotch on the rocks right here, Mr. Devery. Welcome to our town. Though I live in it, I'll say it is real nice."

One of the men at the end of the counter suddenly bawled, "If I want another goddamn drink, I'll have another goddamn drink."

"Excuse me, Mr. Devery," and Joe hurried down the counter.

I sipped my Scotch as I regarded the two men at the far end of the counter. One was short and skinny in his late forties. The other—the one who had bawled—was tall, beefy with a beer paunch and a red, sweating nondescript face that sported a thick Charlie Chan black moustache. He was wearing a light weight dark blue suit, a white shirt and a red tie. He looked to me like a not too successful travelling salesman.

"Joe! Gimme another Scotch!" he bawled. "C'on! Another Scotch!"

"Not if you're going to drive home, Frank," Joe said firmly. "You've had more than enough already."

"Who said I was driving? Tom's going to drive me home."

"That I am not!" the skinny man said sharply. "Do you imagine I want an eight mile walk back to my place?"

"Do you good," the big man said. "Gimme another Scotch, Joe, then we'll go."

"I'm not driving you," Tom said, "and I mean that!"

"Why you skinny sonofabitch, I thought you were my friend!"

"So I am, but I'm not walking eight miles even for a friend."

Listening to all this, something nudged me. Fate's elbow? I wandered down the counter.

" Maybe, gentlemen, I could help," I said.

The big man turned and glared at me.

" Who the hell are you?"

" Now, Frank, that's not polite," Joe said soothingly. " This is Mr. Devery, our new driving instructor. He works for Bert."

The big man peered blearily at me.

" So what's he want?"

I looked at the skinny man.

" If you drive him home, I'll follow and take you back."

The skinny man grabbed my hand and pumped it up and down.

" That's real nice of you, Mr. Devery. Solves the problem. I'm Tom Mason. This is Frank Marshall."

The big man tried to focus me, nodded, then turned to Joe.

" How about that drink?"

Joe poured a shot while Mason plucked at Marshall's sleeve.

" Come on, Frank, it's getting late."

As Marshall downed the drink, I said to Joe, " Would you call Mrs. Hansen and tell her I'll be a little late for dinner?"

" Sure, Mr. Devery. It's real nice of you."

Unsteadily, Marshall strode out of the bar. Mason, shaking his head, followed with me.

" He doesn't know when to stop, Mr. Devery," he muttered. " Such a shame."

He and Marshall got into a shabby looking green Plymouth parked outside the bar. They waited until I got in my car, then Mason drove off. I followed.

Leaving Main street, the Plymouth headed inland. After a ten minute drive we reached what I guessed to be the best residential quarter to judge by the opulent houses and villas, set in well cared for gardens, ablaze with flowers. Another ten minute drive brought us to forests and isolated farmhouses.

The Plymouth's trafficator warned me Mason was turning left. The car disappeared up a narrow dirt road just wide enough for one car. We finally reached a dead-end and there stood a big two-storey house, completely isolated and half hidden by trees and shrubs.

As Mason drove into the short driveway and then into a garage close to the house, I pulled up and reversed the car for the run back. I lit a cigarette and waited. After some five minutes, Tom Mason came hurrying down the drive to join me.

As he got in the car, he said, " This is real nice of you, Mr. Devery. I've known Frank Marshall since we were at school together. He's a nice fella when he isn't in drink. He's frustrated, Mr. Devery, and I can't say I blame him."

" Oh?" I wasn't particularly interested. " What's his trouble then?"

" He's waiting for his aunt to die."

I looked at him, startled.

" Is that right?"

" That's it. He has expectations. He's her heir. Once she passes on, he'll be the richest man in Wicksteed."

Remembering the opulent houses I had passed on the way up, my interest sharpened.

" I'm a newcomer here, Mr. Mason. I wouldn't know how rich that would be." It was carefully phrased. It could produce information, yet didn't indicate I was fishing.

" Between you and me, when she goes, he'll inherit a shade over a million dollars."

I stiffened. My attention became riveted to what he was saying.

" Is that a fact? There's an old saying about waiting for dead men's shoes . . ."

" That's his trouble. The old lady is dying by inches . . . cancer. She could go tomorrow or she could live for sometime. Two years back, she told him she was going to leave him all her money. Since then he has been counting the hours. He's worrying so much about when she's going to die he's begun to hit the bottle. Before she told him, he scarcely touched hard liquor."

21

" Quite a situation, Mr. Mason."

He put his hand on my arm.

" Call me Tom. What's your first name, friend?"

" Keith."

" A family name, huh? It's unusual." He scratched his chin, then went on, " Yes, it sure is a situation, Keith. I'm sorry for him, and I'm sorry for his wife although I've never met her."

" What does he do for a living?"

" He runs a real estate business in 'Frisco. He commutes every day by train."

" Does he do all right?"

" Well, he did, but since he began drinking, he's complaining about the business." Mason shook his head. " But you can't tell Frank a thing. The times I've warned him about his drinking. Let's hope he'll get the money soon, then maybe, he'll pull himself together."

I was now only half listening. As I drove back to Wicksteed, my mind was busy. A shade over a million! Who would believe anyone in such a one horse town could inherit such a sum.

I was suddenly envious. If only I were in Frank Marshall's place! I wouldn't take to the bottle in frustration. With my know-how, I would raise credit on my expectations. I would . . .

My heart gave a little jump.

Was this, I asked myself, the opportunity I had been waiting for so patiently?

two

AFTER DINNER, I went on to the veranda and thought about what Tom Mason had told me. He could, of course, have been exaggerating, but supposing he hadn't been and it was a fact that Marshall was going to inherit a million dollars?

For more than five years, I had been waiting for the opportunity to get my hands on real money. Now, suddenly, in this one horse town, the opportunity appeared to present itself.

The average man, learning that a small time estate agent was coming into a million dollars would think: ' good luck to him ' and then give it no further thought. Certainly the average man wouldn't even begin to think it might be possible to grab Marshall's inheritance, but then I am not the average man.

During my stay in jail, I had shared a cell with a slick con man who liked to boast about his past swindles. He had had, according to him, a spectacular career until he had become too greedy.

" For years, buster," he said to me, " I have traded on other people's greed and then, goddamn it, if I didn't get greedy myself and look where it's landed me . . . ten years in a cell!"

He had expanded on the subject of greed.

" If a guy has two dollars, he will want four. If he has five thousand, he'll want ten. This is human nature. I knew a guy who was worth five million and he nearly bust a gut turning it into seven. The human race is never satisfied. The more they

23

have, the more they want, and if you can show them how to make a fast buck without working for it, they'll be all over you."

From my experience when working with tycoons, I knew this to be true. Marshall's inheritance wouldn't be lying around in leather bags for some smart thief to steal. The money would be in stocks and bonds, guarded by bankers and brokers, but bankers and brokers didn't awe me. I had been a broker myself.

If I were certain that Marshall would inherit a million then with my know-how I was willing to bet I could talk him into an investment that would transfer his million to me. The fact that he was a drunk made it that much easier. I was confident I could talk him into something that would dazzle him: how to turn his million safely into three million.

The human race is never satisfied.

I would use this truth to get his money. It would, of course, have to be a carefully planned operation. I thought of all the files I had kept when working with Barton Sharman and which I had stored in New York. They contained facts, figures, plans and maps from which I could draw on to support any scheme I put before Marshall. That was no problem, but before I could even consider what particular bait to dangle before him, I needed to confirm that he was going to inherit this sum and to have more information about his background. Mason had mentioned that Marshall was married. I would need to know about his wife; if he had children or if he had relations: those tricky people who would help a drunk to safeguard the million when it was his.

I would have to get friendly with Marshall. It was possible, in drink, he might give me this information, although from what I had seen of him, he could be difficult to handle.

After I had finished my day's work, I told myself, I should make a habit of dropping in for a drink at Joe's bar. In this way, I could expand my social contacts and maybe meet Marshall again.

I felt for the first time since I had been released from jail animated and excited. Even if it didn't work out, at least, it gave me something to aim at : my second attempt to make big money !

I got to the Driving school the following morning at ten minutes to nine. Bert was already there, opening the mail.

After we had exchanged greetings, he said, " I hear you gave Tom Mason a helping hand last night."

News certainly travelled fast in Wicksteed ! All the more reason why I must be careful in my inquiries.

" Oh . . . that." I sat on the edge of his desk. " Mason seems a nice guy. He tells me he owns the hardware store here."

" He took it over from his dad who took it over from his dad. Yes, Tom's a nice fella." Bert slit open an envelope. " I wish I could say the same for Frank Marshall. I remember the time when he was all right . . . he'd do anything for you. But now . . ." He shook his head.

" That house of his is pretty isolated," I said. " I wouldn't like to live so far out. It must be tough on his wife."

" You're right, Keith." Bert sat back in his chair. " Marshall's rich aunt left him the house. She used to live in it before she was moved to the hospital. He could have sold it. She wouldn't have cared, but he reckons if he hangs on to it the land around there will be developed and then he'll get a real fancy price for it."

" Tom said he was in real estate." I noted Tom didn't rise to the ' wife bait ' I had thrown out. I decided not to press it.

" That's right. He was doing well a couple of years back, but this drinking of his . . ." Bert frowned. " No one can drink the way he does and expect to run a business."

Maisie came in to tell me my first pupil was waiting.

" See you, Bert," I said and went out to meet a teenage girl with a brace on her teeth and a non-stop giggle.

The morning and afternoon passed quickly. On three occasions, my pupils drove me along Main street and we passed Deputy sheriff Ross. The first time, I lifted my hand in his direction, but he ignored me. The other times I ignored him, but I was aware he was staring at me with those narrow cop's eyes, a bleak expression on his hatchet face.

I would have to be careful of him, I told myself. If I was going to get Marshall's money—always providing he got it himself—the operation was going to be even more tricky with Ross looming in the background, but that didn't fazz me. It would be a challenge, and I was in the mood to accept a challenge.

At 18.00, I said good night to Bert and Maisie, then went over to Joe's bar.

There were only five men in the bar, talking earnestly together. I wondered if Marshall would show.

Joe came down the counter and shook hands.

" What'll it be, Mr. Devery?"

" I think a gin and tonic."

He served the drink, then propped himself up against the counter and seemed ready to talk.

" You weren't too late for your supper last night?"

" No, and thanks for calling Mrs. Hansen."

" That was the least I could do." He shook his head. " That Marshall . . . it's a real shame. I expect Tom told you about him."

" He did mention something about an old aunt."

" That's correct. She used to be a Miss Hackett, a nurse at our hospital . . . a fine lady. One day, there was an accident : a bad car smash and the driver got taken to our hospital. This was some forty years ago. I was a nipper at school at the time, but my dad told me about it. The injured man turned out to be Howard T. Fremlin of Pittsburg. He owned the Fremlin Steel Corporation. He was passing through to 'Frisco on a business trip when this truck hit him. To cut a long story short, Miss Hackett, after nursing him for quite a time, married him. It was only when he died, some thirty years later, that she returned to Wicksteed and bought that big house where Marshall now lives. Now she's real bad in hospital where she once worked. Funny the way things work out, isn't it?"

I said it was. I sipped my drink, then said, " Tom said it was cancer."

" Correct . . . Leukaemia. It's a wonder they've kept her alive for so long, but now, I hear she could go any moment."

" Fremlin?" I squinted at my drink. " Some sort of millionaire, wasn't he?"

" Correct. He left her a cool million which Marshall is going to inherit. The rest of Fremlin's estate went to charities. I heard it was around ten million."

" That's money." I now had confirmation that Tom Mason hadn't been exaggerating and I decided to shift the conversation to Joe's son, Sammy. As I was saying that Sammy would have to have a few more lessons, a big, bulky man came into the bar. I glanced at him, then stiffened. He was wearing the fawn shirt, the dark brown slacks and the fawn Stetson of a cop.

He paused at my side and shook hands with Joe.

" Howdy, Sam," Joe said. " What'll it be?"

" A beer."

The big man half turned and looked at me. He was around fifty-five with alert grey eyes, a droopy moustache, a jutting chin and a nose that looked as if someone had taken a poke at it at one time. On his shirt was a badge which read : Sheriff Sam McQueen.

" Meet Mr. Devery, Sam," Joe said as he poured the beer. " Bert's new driving instructor."

" Howdy." McQueen offered his hand.

We shook hands. There was a pause, then McQueen said, " I've been hearing about you, Mr. Devery. Let's sit down. I've been on my feet all day." Carrying his beer, he walked over to a far table.

I hesitated, then looked at Joe.

" A real nice guy," Joe whispered. " One of the best."

I picked up my drink and joined McQueen at the table. He offered me a cigar.

" Thanks, but I don't smoke them," I said and lit a cigarette.

" Welcome to Wicksteed." He paused to drink half his beer, sighed, slapped his paunch and set down his glass. " This is a nice little town." He lit his cigar, then went on, " I'll tell you something. Our crime rate is the lowest on the Pacific coast."

" That's something to sing about," I said.

" I guess. Apart from some kids stealing from the store, a few drunks, kids borrowing other people's cars from time to time is all. No serious crime, Mr. Devery. Makes me a little lazy, but I don't mind being lazy. At my age, it's nice not to have to race and chase."

I nodded.

There was a long pause, then McQueen said quietly, " I hear you had a run-in with my young deputy."

Here it comes, I thought and braced myself. Keeping my expression wooden, I said, " He thought I was stealing Mr. Ryder's car."

McQueen took another drink.

" He's a very ambitious boy. A mite too ambitious. I'm hoping to get him transferred to 'Frisco where the action is. Without my say-so, he checked on you and gave me a report."

I looked through the open doorway at the home going traffic crawling along in the hot sun. I felt a little chill run through me.

" Having read the report, Mr. Devery, I thought I'd better check for myself." McQueen paused to blow smoke. " That's my job. I talked to Ryder, Pinner and Mason. I also talked to Mrs. Hansen. I told them I wanted to know what they thought of you, you being a stranger here and as they know, strangers are my business. They all gave you a remarkably good report. From what they tell me you could become a useful citizen here. I heard you helped Mason to get Marshall home. I hear you handled young Hank Sobers well, and I've had trouble with him in the past. I know he needs handling."

I didn't say anything. I waited.

He finished his beer.

" I've got to move along. The wife's got roast chicken for supper and I don't want to be late. You're welcome here. Pay no attention to Ross. I've told him not to bother you." He looked straight at me, his eyes twinkling. " The fact is, Mr. Devery, I believe in letting sleeping dogs lie. No one in this town is going to make trouble for you if you don't make trouble for yourself. Fair enough?"

" Fair enough, Sheriff," I said, my mouth a little dry.

He got to his feet, shook hands, waved to Joe and walked out onto the street.

As Joe had said : a real nice guy : one of the best, but I knew enough about cops to be sure, in spite of the welcome speech, he would keep an eye on me. He would be a fool if he didn't, and one thing I was sure of : Sheriff McQueen was nobody's fool.

Joe came over to pick up the empty beer glass.

" The thing I like about Sam is his friendliness," he said as he wiped the table with a swab. " He's been Sheriff here for close on twenty years. He makes a point of knowing everyone and getting on with them. Not like Deputy Ross who is looking for trouble all the time. I hear Ross is going to be transferred when there is a vacancy in 'Frisco . . . the sooner the better."

" Mr. Marshall not in tonight?" I asked casually.

" He doesn't come here much and then only with Tom because he expects Tom to drive him home. No, Marshall does his drinking at home. He's no fool. The last thing he wants is to lose his driving licence. He'd really be in a fix without a car, living where he does."

Here was my chance.

" Doesn't his wife drive?"

Joe shrugged.

" I wouldn't know, Mr. Devery. I've never set eyes on her. She never comes into town."

" Is that right? Must be lonely for her out there."

" It's a funny thing but some women like being on their own," Joe said. " You take my wife. She spends all her time either gardening or staring at the tube. She's not sociable like me."

Two men came in and Joe hurried to serve them. I finished my drink, then waving to him, I went out into the hot sun and to my car.

That evening, after dinner, I sat on the veranda and mulled over the information I had gained. It did look as if Marshall was to inherit a million dollars. The fact that his aunt had been left a million by her husband gave substance to both Mason's and Joe's gossip. But how was I to be absolutely certain that she was going to leave all this money to Marshall? I would have to get more solid information before I began to think seriously about the operation.

I thought too about the Sheriff. He now knew my record. This, I told myself, after thinking about it, was inevitable. Sooner or later, he would have found out and it seemed to me it was better sooner than later. If Marshall's money suddenly disappeared and McQueen only then discovered there was an ex-jailbird in this town, his suspicions would naturally centre on me, but knowing my record long before I began my operation, his suspicions might not be so concentrated.

I was interested in the scrap of information Joe had given me about Marshall's wife. So she was a loner. I would need to know more about her before I could make a plan.

I went to bed that night, satisfied I had begun well. As I settled to sleep, I told myself I had to be patient. A million dollars was worth waiting for.

*   *   *

I learned nothing new about Marshall during the next three days. I avoided asking questions when talking to Bert and Joe. Marshall's name didn't come up and although I was tempted, I didn't bring it up myself.

On the fourth morning, when Mrs. Hansen came up with my breakfast, I got a break, although, at the time I didn't know it.

" Could I ask you a favour, Mr. Devery?" she said as she put down the tray.

" Why, of course."

" My sister with her husband lives on a farm and every so often she sends me farm produce. She is sending me two ducks by rail. I don't trust the rail people to deliver at once. I wouldn't want the birds to spoil in this hot weather. They'll be on the six-twenty from 'Frisco. Could I ask you to be so kind as to collect them for me?"

" Why sure. No problem."

" Just tell Mr Haines, the stationmaster, you're collecting them for me and many thanks, Mr Devery."

After the day's work, I drove to the railroad station. Leaving the car in the parking lot, I walked into the station and found Mr Haines, a bent, white-haired little man, on the platform.

I introduced myself, telling him I was to collect a parcel for Mrs. Hansen. He squinted at me, nodded and shook hands.

" I've heard about you, Mr. Devery. You're teaching my granddaughter to drive . . . Emma Haines. How's she doing?"

I remembered Emma. She was the one with the brace and the giggles.

" She's making progress, Mr. Haines, but she'll need a few more lessons."

" That's all the kids think about these days." He shook his head. " Rushing around in cars." He took out an old fashioned watch. " Due in any moment now, Mr. Devery. I'll get the package for you."

He went off down the far end of the platform. As I lit a cigarette, I spotted Deputy sheriff Ross getting out of a police car. He walked with slow strides to the car park, then propped his lean figure against a car fender.

I turned as I heard the train approaching. It slid slowly to a halt and people began to spill out, all moving fast to the parking lot. Mr. Haines approached, carrying a box.

" Here you are, Mr. Devery. Just sign here." As I was sign-ing I saw Frank Marshall getting off the train. He got off like

31

a man descending a dangerous slope on Mount Everest. I could see he was plastered to the eyeballs. A bottle of Scotch was sagging out of his jacket pocket. His face was a fiery red and sweat made black patches on his pale blue suit. He was the last passenger off the train. He came unsteadily towards me as Mr. Haines went into his office.

Marshall squinted at me as he passed, but he didn't seem to recognise me. Then I remembered that Deputy sheriff Ross was outside. I put down the box and caught hold of Marshall's arm.

" Mr. Marshall . . ."

" Huh?" He turned and stared blearily at me.

" We met in Joe's bar. I'm Devery."

" So what?" He pulled away from me. " So what's so important about that?"

" I thought you'd better know Deputy sheriff Ross is outside."

Marshall frowned. I saw he was trying to concentrate.

"That sonofabitch . . . who cares about him?" he said doubtfully.

" That's up to you, Mr. Marshall. I thought you might like to know," and turning, I picked up the box.

" Hey! Wait!"

I paused.

" What's he doing out there?" Marshall asked, peering at me.

" Waiting for you I imagine."

He thought about this, swaying drunkenly, then slowly nodded.

" Yeah . . . he could at that, the bastard." He pushed his hat to the back of his head and blotted his face with his handkerchief. " Maybe I shouldn't have had that little drink on the train." He nodded. " Yeah, maybe I shouldn't have."

Here was an opportunity I wasn't going to miss.

" Suppose I drive you home, Mr. Marshall? I have the time."

He put his head on one side and stared.

" That's pretty white of you, friend. Would you do that?"

" Sure."

He screwed up his eyes while he tried to think.

" How will you get back?" he finally asked.

I was surprised he even considered that.

" No problem. I'll walk."

Marshall bunched his hand into a fist and tapped me on the chest.

" That's real neighbourly. Okay, friend, let's go. Tell you what . . . have dinner with us. That's a quid pro quo. You have dinner with us."

Carrying the box, I walked with him out of the station and towards the parking lot.

As we reached Marshall's Plymouth, Deputy sheriff Ross appeared.

" You driving, Mr. Marshall?" he demanded, his narrow eyes flickering from Marshall to me.

" My friend is driving," Marshall said with drunken dignity. " Why should you care?"

Ross turned to me.

" You leaving your car here?"

" Any law against it, Deputy sheriff?" I asked, getting into the Plymouth.

Marshall exploded into a haw-haw-haw, then lurched around the car and slumped into the passenger's seat. I drove away, leaving Ross staring after us the way a tiger would stare, seeing a fat roebuck speeding to safety.

" That's screwed the sonofabitch," Marshall said and slapped me on my knee. " He's been laying for me for months, but I'm too smart for him."

" All the same, Mr. Marshall, you should be more careful."

" You think so?" He peered at me. " Yeah, maybe you're right. Now, I'll tell you something. Before long, I'm going to own this little town. I'm going to be the Big shot here and I'll see Ross gets kicked the hell off the force."

" Is that right, Mr. Marshall?" I was now driving along Main street.

" Cut the mister. I'm Frank to my friends. What's your first name, friend?"

" Keith."

" That's some name. Where are you from?"

" New York."

I turned left and headed towards Mrs. Hansen's house.

" You like New York?"

" Can't say I do."

" Nor do I. I don't like 'Frisco either, but that's where I have to earn a living, but not for long. I'm going to have so much money, Keith, I'll be able to buy up this little town."

I pulled up outside Mrs. Hansen's house.

" I live here, Frank. I've got to drop off this box. I won't be a minute."

As I entered the front hall with the box, Mrs. Hansen met me.

" Here it is, Mrs. Hansen. I'm sorry . . . I won't be in for dinner. I have a problem."

She looked beyond me through the open front door and saw Marshall sitting in the Plymouth.

" Oh! Are you taking the poor man home, Mr. Devery?"

" That's it. He's invited me to dinner."

" But how will you get back without your car?"

" I'll walk." I smiled at her. " I'm used to walking," and leaving her, I returned to the Plymouth.

Marshall had fallen asleep, his bulk wedged against the off-side door, his mouth hanging open. He slept all the way to his house. My memory served me well and I had no trouble finding my way.

I pulled up before the front door, then gently shook Marshall's arm.

" We're home, Frank," I said.

He didn't stir.

I gave him a harder shake, but it was like shaking a corpse.

After a third try, I got out of the car and walked up the five broad steps to the front door. I thumbed the bell push and waited.

I was feeling tense. Here was my chance to meet Mrs. Marshall and I badly wanted to meet her. I wanted to judge the kind of woman she was and to judge if she could be a danger if and when I began the operation.

It was hot out there on the top step with the evening sun burning down on me. After a wait, I rang again. No one came to the door. I rang a third time : still no one came.

Exasperated, I stepped back and looked up at the row of windows of the upper storey. One of the curtains moved slightly. So she was there, but she wasn't going to open up. I returned to the car and shook Marshall again. He slid further down in his seat and began to snore.

So . . . no Mrs. Marshall and no dinner, but only an eight-mile walk back to Wicksteed.

I wasn't discouraged. I had made good progress this evening. Marshall was now in debt to me. We were on Christian name terms and he had told me he was going to be rich.

I had yet to meet the elusive Mrs. Marshall, but there was time.

Leaving Marshall snoring in his car, I walked down the drive and down the long dirt road towards Wicksteed.

*　　*　　*

The next morning was Saturday. Bert had told me Saturday was the busiest day of the week. It was on Saturday pupils were tested to see if they were good enough to take the official test.

I had just finished dressing when Mrs. Hansen brought in the breakfast tray.

" I hope you weren't too tired after that long walk, Mr. Devery," she said setting down the tray. " It must be a good eight miles."

" I was lucky. I got a lift," I told her and I had. A truck

driver had picked me up at the bottom of the dirt road and had taken me back to Wicksteed.

" Then I hope you had a good dinner."

" I missed out on the dinner. Mr. Marshall was asleep and Mrs. Marshall wasn't at home."

" Well, I am surprised. From what I hear, Mrs. Marshall stays home." She paused, then went on, " Would you care to have Sunday lunch with us, Mr. Devery? Only my brother and myself. Would you like that?"

Surprised, I thanked her and said I would be pleased to join them.

I had had no idea she had a brother, and casually, I mentioned to Bert that I was lunching with her and her brother.

" That'll be Yule Olson," Bert said. " He's our only solicitor. He handles all the family business in this town. You'll like him. He's a nice fella."

I wondered if Olson handled Marshall's affairs : better still Marshall's aunt's affairs.

The day's work went reasonably well. I had to advise two of my pupils to have more lessons before attempting the test and Bert had to fail three on the code.

At the end of the day, we had a drink together in his office and he paid me the hundred dollars due to me.

" We don't work Mondays, Keith," he said. " I believe in a five-day week. What are you planning to do?"

I shrugged.

" I have this Sunday lunch with Mrs. Hansen. I guess after I'll go on the beach."

He eyed me thoughtfully.

" Do you think you're going to find it lonely here?"

I shook my head.

" I'm used to being on my own." Lowering my voice in case Maisie, in the other room, might hear, I went on, " When you have been in jail as long as I have, loneliness doesn't worry you."

" You could think about getting married. There are lots of nice girls around here."

" I can't afford to get married."

He took off his glasses and began to polish them.

"Yes . . . two hundred isn't much, but if you like the work . . ." He paused, then put on his glasses to look directly at me. " I'm not getting any younger. I've taken a liking to you, Keith. I've decided to make the same offer to you as I once made my son."

I shifted in my chair, wondering what was coming.

" My son had big ideas," Bert went on. " He wasn't interested in my offer. I offered him a fifty-fifty partnership. It was, and still is worth five hundred a week. The idea was for me to retire and he take over. I would dabble a little in the business, but he would have the running of it." A long pause, then he went on, " I'm offering you the same proposition."

I stared at him.

" That's really good of you, Bert, but you're far too young to retire."

He smirked.

" I'm seventy-two and I want to pull out. I want to spend more time in my garden. I could come in twice a week to take care of the code classes, but you would handle the rest of the business. When Tom Lucas gets out of hospital, he could handle the driving lessons, you the office. You think about it. You could do worse."

" Are you serious about this, Bert?"

He nodded.

" Don't look so surprised. I reckon I'm a good judge of men. You could make a real go of this. If you want it, you can take over at the end of the year."

Who would want a small-time Driving school, I thought, when there was a million to be grabbed?

" Appreciate this a lot, Bert," I said. " If you really mean it, I'll certainly think about it. There's no immediate rush, is there?"

I saw a flash of disappointment in his eyes. He probably imagined I would jump at his offer.

" No, there's no rush. You think about it. If I could have persuaded my son to come in with me, I had ideas about setting up a U-drive service and even a Travel agency. They all go together. With an energetic fella like you, and me supplying the capital, it could work out good. You think about it."

" I certainly will." I didn't want to hurt him, so I added, " It's just that I'm used to big cities. I'm not sure if I could settle in such a small town. That's my problem. I think I might . . . I just want to convince myself."

He looked happier then.

But I didn't think about it. My sights were set much higher than to spend the rest of my days in a one-horse town like Wicksteed. I wanted to get into the big league where the real money was.

By the time I got back to my room I had even forgotten about Bert's offer . . . that was how disinterested I was.

I spent the rest of the evening after dinner watching the fights on the tube. They were pretty bad and I only half concentrated. I was impatient for lunch time tomorrow when I would meet Yule Olson.

*   *   *

When I entered Mrs. Hansen's living-room, I found Yule Olson already there. He was sitting on the patio, sipping a weak whisky and water and reading the Sunday newspaper.

Mrs. Hansen led me out onto the patio and made the introductions.

Olson was around fifty-five : a tall, thin, balding man with clear blue eyes and a kindly smile. He shook hands and asked if I would like a whisky or there was gin. I elected for a gin and tonic.

" I'll leave you two together," Mrs. Hansen said. " Lunch will be ready in twenty minutes."

I found Olson easy to talk to. We chatted about Wicksteed

and politics until Mrs. Hansen called us to the table.

The ducks were good and I complimented Mrs. Hansen on her cooking. It was while the apple pie was being served that Mrs. Hansen gave me the opening I was hoping for.

" Mr. Devery has been so very kind," she said as she passed the bowl of thick cream. " Twice he has helped poor Frank to get home, and only last Friday, Mr. Devery actually had to walk half the way back."

Olson frowned.

" I haven't seen Frank in weeks. So he's still drinking?" He looked at me. " Was he bad?"

" I guess so. Deputy sheriff Ross was waiting for him so I thought the best thing was to drive him home."

" I hope he thanked you."

" He was sleeping when I left him, but on the way up, he did tell me he was going to be so rich he was going to buy up Wicksteed and he would reward me then." I laughed, making a joke of it.

" He is certainly going to be very rich," Mrs. Hansen said.

" Now, Martha . . ." Olson broke in.

" Don't be silly, Yule. I know he is your client, but it's no secret he is going to inherit the Fremlin millions. Everyone knows that. He has told them enough times."

" A million : not millions," Olson said. " You shouldn't exaggerate."

" He did say something about that," I said casually, " but I didn't believe it. I thought he was rambling."

" No. His aunt is leaving him her fortune, but he hasn't got it yet," Olson said.

" It won't be long now. I visited dear Helen yesterday. She's dreadfully weak." Mrs. Hansen turned to me. " Mrs. Fremlin and I worked together at the hospital when we were girls. She married this steel millionaire and I married the local school-master." She sounded a shade wistful.

" You got the better bargain," Olson said. " Fremlin was a hard man."

"So she is really bad?" I said to keep the conversation moving.

"The poor dear is dying . . . leukaemia," Mrs. Hansen said, her face distressed. "Dr. Chandler told me yesterday it can now be only a matter of weeks."

"Really, Martha, you shouldn't gossip like this," Olson said sharply. "Dr. Chandler has no business to discuss Helen with you."

"Nonsense, Yule! You seem to forget I was once a nurse. Naturally, Dr. Chandler confides in me, knowing I am Helen's closest friend."

"Well, then don't go talking about what Dr. Chandler tells you. It wouldn't surprise me if Helen lasts another year."

"Three or four weeks," Mrs. Hansen said firmly. "Not a day more, and let me tell you, Yule, Dr. Chandler knows what he is talking about and you don't!"

"I suggest we have coffee on the patio," Olson said stiffly, and that ended the argument.

It was while Mrs. Hansen was washing up that Olson said, "If you will excuse me saying so, Mr. Devery, I find it a little odd that a young man of your obvious education should be content to waste his time teaching people to drive."

"I don't consider it a waste of time." I smiled at him. "Someone has to do it . . . so why not me?"

"That doesn't make you very ambitious."

"Who said I was?" I laughed. "Even before I was drafted into the Army, I was happy just to get along, and after Vietnam . . ."

There was a long pause, then he said, "There are a number of good openings in this town for an educated man. For instance, I could use an accountant. My man is retiring. Do you know anything about keeping books, Mr. Devery?"

I realised he was trying to be helpful as Bert Ryder had been trying to be helpful, but I wasn't interested. I was only interested in Marshall's million.

"Not a thing," I lied. "I can scarcely add two and two

together. It is kind of you to think of me, Mr. Olson. Frankly, I'm happy as I am."

He lifted his shoulders in a disappointed shrug.

" Well, don't leave it too late. Take the advice of an older man. Remember that wise saying : a rolling stone . . ."

Mrs. Hansen appeared then, and Olson, looking at his watch, said he had to go to the church. He took the afternoon bible class.

Back in my room, I lay on the bed and considered the information I had acquired. One thing was now certain : Marshall was going to inherit a million dollars, and it also seemed certain that his aunt wasn't going to last more than a few weeks. It looked as if I had arrived on the scene at exactly the right time.

I would have liked to know how this million had been invested and what income it yielded. Olson would know, but I couldn't ask him. Marshall might know, but the chances were he didn't. Still, I might try a gentle probe the next time I met him, but how to meet him unless I met his train? That, I decided, could be dangerously obvious. My mind then switched to Mrs. Marshall.

Before I went to jail, women had shared most of my leisure time. I had been stupid enough to have married a woman eight years older than myself. After a couple of years, I had lost interest in her and had begun to look elsewhere. I discovered lots of willing girls much younger, much more attractive than my wife. After a year of continuous cheating, she finally caught up with me. I couldn't afford a divorce at that time so, after a lot of talk and eating humble pie, I managed to kid her it would never happen again, made the usual promises and eventually convinced her I was on the level and would remain that way. Then I was drafted to Vietnam. I had a ball out there. The Vietnamese girls were as accommodating as they were gorgeous. Back home again, I found life with my wife deadly dull after the night-life in Saigon. Once more I began to cheat, then the merger thing blew up and I went to jail. By then, my wife had had enough of me and had found someone else. She got a divorce. At least, I didn't have to pay alimony.

Apart from a few whores to relieve the pressure, I had kept away from women simply because I couldn't afford to take them around, feed them, take them to movies before I could get into their beds. Now for the first time I wondered if my sex technique might win me something.

From what I had heard, Mrs. Marshall lived like a hermit. Unless she was a nutter, she surely would welcome male attention. It was just possible, if I handled her right, I could get more information from her than from her husband. The problem, of course, was how to contact her.

I had nothing to do on Monday, the following day. Marshall was certain to be in 'Frisco. Suppose, I told myself, I drove up to his house to inquire how he was . . . introducing myself as the good samaritan who had driven him safely back home from the railroad station? Just a neighbourly call. What was the matter with that for an idea?

I thought about it, then decided again it was too obvious. I had to be patient. There was still plenty of time. Until his aunt died and Marshall got the money, I must wait.

Getting off the bed, I put on swim trunks, collected a towel and went down to the beach.

It seemed everyone in Wicksteed had the same idea. I had to pick my way over bodies to get into the sea. I swam amongst screaming, laughing youngsters, fat middle aged women, scraggy middle aged men and a number of real oldies.

This was not my idea of fun.

As I was walking across the sand towards Mrs. Hansen's house, I heard my name called. Looking around, I saw Joe Pinner seated in a deck chair under the shade of a palm tree. He waved to me.

As I walked up to him, he said, " Howdy, friend," and pointed to an empty deck chair by his side. " Rest your legs if you haven't anything better to do."

I sat down beside him.

" The wife's just gone home," he said as if to explain why he was here on his own. " She can't take too much sun. I hear you got fixed up with Bert. How are you liking it?"

" I like it fine, and thanks, Mr. Pinner."

He stroked his Mark Twain moustache, a twinkle in his eyes.

" I told you . . . this is a nice little town: the best on the Pacific coast." He dug into a plastic bag and produced a cigar. " Want one of these?"

" Thanks, no." I had brought along my cigarettes. We lit up and stared at the crowd on the beach.

" Sam McQueen, our sheriff, called on me, asking about you," Pinner said, easing his bulk in the deck chair. " That's his job. He's a fine man. I gave you a good reference. I hear he talked to you."

" Yes . . . he seems a nice guy."

" You can say that again." He blew smoke. " Tom Mason tells me you've been neighbourly. You helped Frank Marshall out of a fix." He eyed me. " Frank needs a lot of help right now. His friends are all rallying around."

I flicked ash off my cigarette.

" Why is he so special, Mr. Pinner?"

" Before very long, he is going to be the most important citizen in this town whether he likes it or not." Pinner frowned at his cigar. " The fact is our Town planning committee—I'm a member—has been hatching an important scheme for some time. Before Mrs. Fremlin got really bad, we put this scheme up to her, but she wasn't interested. I guess when you are as ill as she is, you don't get interested in future schemes, but she told us, when she passed on, she was leaving all her money to her nephew, Frank, and it would be up to him to do what he thought best."

" May I ask what the scheme is, Mr. Pinner?" I asked cautiously.

" Why sure. It's no secret. The one thing we lack in this

town is an amusement park, plus a good hotel. We reckon if we could raise a half a million, we could build an amusement park that would attract a whale of a lot of tourists. This town needs tourists. We already have three hotels here, but they aren't much. We need a hotel that caters for the medium rich. I've guaranteed the committee a hundred thousand. Ten more public spirited citizens will put up fifty thousand each. That takes care of the load, but we want Marshall to put up at least three hundred thousand. Once he agrees, we can really put Wicksteed on the tourist map."

"Sounds a great idea," I said. "How does Frank react?" Pinner pulled at his cigar, frowning.

"That's our problem. I don't have to tell you Frank's a drunk. He gives damn-all about anything except the bottle, but we are working on him. I think we can talk sense into him, given time, but we have to be careful he doesn't do anything foolish. He would be the chairman of our committee once we become operative. He would have to be chairman with his big stake, and knowing Frank, he would insist on being chairman. I and the rest of us keep telling him it's a fine investment, but his argument is he hasn't got the money yet and he'll only begin to think about it when he does get it."

"In the meantime, you can't make plans?"

"That's it. Not only that, the cost of materials keeps rising. While we wait, our scheme becomes more and more costly. Frank could easily raise a loan right now on his expectations. We could begin our planning without waiting for Mrs. Fremlin to pass on if only he would agree, but he's being bull headed about it. He knows he couldn't invest his money better than to sink it in this town, but he's too goddamn drunk these days to talk business. How he manages to run that estate office of his in 'Frisco beats me. His secretary must be doing all the work."

"Quite a problem," I said. "Have you talked to his wife? Some women can influence their husbands. Can't she influence him?"

Pinner snorted.

" None of us has ever met Mrs. Marshall." He tugged at his moustache. " She keeps very much to herself. She hasn't ever come into town. I hear she does the shopping on the phone."

" Do you mean no one here has ever seen her?"

" That's right. According to Frank, he met her in 'Frisco, married her and brought her to live in that big, lonely house. I've talked to him, telling him it isn't right for her to live alone the way she does. Between you and me, she is as important to Wicksteed as Frank is. If anything happened to him, she would get his money. It would be a hell of a thing if she collected that million and then walked out on this town. That's what worries us. That's why we keep urging the ladies here to try to contact her and that's why we are also keeping an eye on Frank."

" What did he say when you talked to him about his wife?"

" He just laughed." Pinner made a gesture of disgust. " He said his wife liked being on her own and for the ladies to mind their own business."

" Has he been married long?"

" Three years . . . before he started to drink."

" I suppose there are no children?"

" No children and no relations. He's the last of the Marshalls. He did have a sister, but she died a few years back. No, if anything happened to him, his wife would get the lot." He stubbed out his cigar in the sand. " Since you saved him from that sonofabitch Ross, we have been talking about what's best to do. We now have arranged to meet the train every evening to make sure Frank is fit to drive home. We've made up a roster. There's Tom Mason, Harry Jacks, Fred Selby and me. We are going to take it in turns to be at the station. We reckon Frank will appreciate being taken care of and he could reciprocate by listening to reason."

" It'll be a bit rough on whoever it is to have to walk back eight miles," I said, " but maybe you think it's all in a good cause."

" No one's walking back," Pinner said. " We've got this

45

organised. Whoever takes him back will telephone and one of us will go out and pick him up."

"Is it that important?" I asked, staring out to sea.

"Yeah. It wouldn't help if Olson tries to raise a loan on Frank's expectations for the bank to find out Frank is a drunk. Apart from that, he might kill himself in his car."

"Yes." I paused, then went on, "I haven't anything to do in the evenings. Suppose I help out? I could meet him at the station any night that would fit in with your roster."

He clapped a heavy hand on my knee.

"That's what I call real neighbourly. How about Tuesday nights? Tom is doing the Monday stint. If you get stuck out there, you call Tom and he'll pick you up. If he gets stuck, he'll call you. How's about it?"

"That's fine with me."

As I walked back to Mrs. Hansen's house, I decided Wick-steed's planning committee was just as anxious to get its greedy hands on Marshall's money as I was, but I preferred my chances to theirs.

three

Joe Pinner's scheme to protect Marshall from a drink-drive charge exploded as I walked into the hall of Mrs. Hansen's house.

She came fluttering out of the living-room, obviously in distress.

"Oh, Mr. Devery, I'm so glad you're back!" she exclaimed. "Mr. McQueen is trying to contact my brother. There is no telephone in the church. Could I ask you to help?"

"Why, sure. What is it?"

"It's Mr. Marshall. He has had a car accident."

Here it is, I thought. The drunk has dropped into the grave he has been digging for himself.

"Is he hurt?"

"No . . . I don't think so, but he is under arrest. Mr. McQueen said it will be a drink-drive and assault charge and my brother should be there. Isn't it terrible?"

"Where is the church, Mrs. Hansen?"

"It's on Pinewood avenue. The first turning on the left at the end of this road."

"I'll get your brother."

I ran up the stairs, threw on a sweat shirt and slacks and then pounded down to my car.

I found Olson coming from the church, surrounded by kids.

47

When he saw me, he waved the kids away and joined me as I got out of the car.

" Sheriff McQueen is asking for you, Mr. Olson," I said. " Marshall is in trouble . . . a drink-drive and assault charge. He's now at the station house."

For a brief moment, Olson lost his cool. His eyes popped wide open, then he recovered himself and became all lawyer.

" Thank you, Mr. Devery. How unfortunate."

This, I thought, was the understatement of the week.

" It sure is," I said.

" I'll go at once."

I watched him drive away, then seeing a call booth by the church, I went in, found Joe Pinner's number in the book and called him.

" This is Devery," I said when he came on the line. " Marshall is in trouble. He's facing a drink-drive and assault charge. He's at the station house right now and Olson is on his way."

" Sweet suffering Pete!" Pinner moaned. " I'll get over there. Thanks, Devery," and he hung up.

It occurred to me that it wouldn't do me any harm to spread the news further. So I looked up Tom Mason's home number and broke the news to him.

He reacted the same way as Pinner had done.

" Good grief!" he exclaimed. " I'll get down there right away. Will you join me, Keith?"

I played it modest.

" Why, sure, if you think I can be of use."

" All Frank's friends should be there," Mason said. " This is serious."

Yet another great understatement.

I said I would be there.

When I arrived outside the station house, a big crowd was milling around. Three newsmen and four photographers were on the scene like vultures waiting for a meal.

Joe Pinner, a cigar stuck in his face, was standing by his black Caddy. I walked over to him.

"What goes on, Mr. Pinner?" I asked.

He pushed his Stetson to the back of his head.

"Olson is handling it." He dragged at his Mark Twain moustache. "What a goddamn mess just when we thought we had it organised! Tom is in there, talking to McQueen." He paused, rolled his cigar around in his mouth, then added, "Tom is McQueen's cousin. He has a pull."

We stood around as the crowd built up.

"This is a hell of a thing," Pinner said after a while. "The press will give it a spread and the publicity could sink our loan."

Never mind Marshall, all he was worrying about was the loan.

Tom Mason came through the crowd and joined us. The newsmen surged forward and flashlights popped. There was a yell for a statement. Obviously enjoying his moment of importance, Tom waved them away.

"You guys talk to the Sheriff. I've got no comment." He caught hold of Pinner's arm and pulled him towards Pinner's car. I drifted along with them.

"That was real good of you, Keith, to have called me," Tom said. "Let's get in and I'll give you the set-up."

We got in the car. Pinner turned on the air conditioner and wound up the windows. A small crowd milled around, staring in at us.

"How bad is it?" Pinner asked as he settled his bulk behind the driving wheel. I was sitting at the back.

"Couldn't be worse," Tom said. "This afternoon, Frank drove to the hospital to see his aunt. According to him, he was so upset by her condition, he had to have a little drink. You know what that means. He probably knocked back half a bottle. Anyway, that sonofabitch Ross was waiting for him. I guess Frank lost his head and he took a poke at Ross. He knocked out a couple of teeth."

" Sweet grief ! " Pinner moaned.

" You can say that again." Mason shook his head. " Olson is trying to fix it with Sam, but it's tricky because Ross is yelling blue murder. He wants Frank in jail."

" They wouldn't do that ? " Pinner looked horrified. " If Frank goes to jail, the loan is sunk."

" Yeah, and Sam knows it. He's as interested as we are. The way he is talking to Olson, I reckon there's going to be a fix. I guess the worst that can happen is Frank will lose his licence to drive."

" Who the hell cares ? " Pinner snapped. " But you're sure he won't go to jail ? "

" If Sam can take care of Ross, he won't, but it's not going to be easy."

There came a tapping on the car window. A cop was beckoning to me. I stared at him, then lowered the window.

" You Devery ? " he demanded.

" Yes."

" Mr. Olson wants you."

I looked at Pinner and then at Mason who were staring at the cop.

" What goes on ? " Pinner demanded, lowering his window.

" I wouldn't know," the cop said indifferently. " Mr. Olson said to fetch this guy and that's what I'm doing."

" You'd better go, Keith," Mason said.

" Sure."

I got out of the car and walked with the cop to the station house. I had to shove my way through the gaping crowd, the newsmen and through a barrage of flashlights.

I was led into the Sheriff's office where Olson, McQueen and Marshall were sitting around a desk.

After a quick look at Olson and McQueen, I turned my attention to Marshall. He was dozing and I could see he was pretty drunk.

Olson said, " Frank . . . Mr. Devery is here."

Marshall shook his head, opened his eyes, peered at me, shut them, opened them again and then grinned.

" Hi, Keith ! I want you to drive me home."

I looked from him to McQueen who gave a resigned nod. Then I looked at Olson who also nodded.

" If you would be so kind, Mr. Devery," Olson said. " I have taken care of the formalities." Turning to Marshall, he went on, " All right, Frank, I'll see you tomorrow."

" Unless I see you first," Marshall said and heaved himself to his feet. He staggered, then grabbed hold on my shoulder. " Screw the lot of you," he said, then to me, " Come on, pal. Let's get the hell out of here."

I went with him into the hot sun. The moment we appeared, the newsmen surged forward, and there was a murmur from the crowd.

Marshall was impressive. He was like a whale among the minnows. Shoving his way through the crowd, muttering four-letter words, he reached my car and got in. I could see Pinner and Tom Mason gaping. I slid under the driving wheel, started the motor amid blinding flash explosions.

I drove away and headed towards Marshall's house. I kept checking my driving mirror, but no one was following us.

Marshall slumped against the off-side door and every now and then he snored.

When we finally reached the bottom of the dirt road leading to the house, he came awake.

" Anyone following us, Keith?"

I checked my driving mirror.

" We're on our own."

" Let's stop."

I swung the car to the grass verge and cut the motor.

" I'm in trouble, Keith. They are going to take my driving licence away . . . the creeps can't do anything else." He rubbed his hand over his sweating face. " At least, I hit that bastard. He had it coming. The joke is they're scared to do anything about that." He closed his eyes and nodded off. I sat behind the driving wheel and watched him. After a few minutes he yawned, stretched and then looked at me.

" Until that old bitch dies," he said, " and she's taking a hell of a time doing it, I've got to earn a living. If I can't drive, I'm in trouble." He leaned back, puffed out his cheeks and then went on, " It's time Beth—that's my wife—did something for me." He turned his head and squinted at me. " Will you teach her to drive?"

This was just too easy.

" That's my job, Frank . . . teaching people to drive."

He dropped a sweaty hand on my wrist.

" That's right. So . . . you teach her to drive, so she can get me to the station." He wiped his face with his handkerchief, then said, " Excuse me," and opening the car door, he lurched out and vomited on the grass verge. I watched him. To me he represented a million dollars. Why should I care if he behaved worse than an animal?

After a while, he staggered back into the car, wiping his mouth on his coat sleeve.

" I guess I had one drink too many." He sank back in the seat, then he patted my arm. " When I get that money, I'm going to be the Big shot around here and I'll remember my friends." He blew out his cheeks, then went on, " Let's get home."

I drove up the dirt road and parked outside the front entrance of the house. He heaved himself out of the car and stood swaying, while he looked at me through the open window.

" I'm still a bit drunk, Keith, but tomorrow I'll call you." He waved. " Thanks, pal."

I watched him stagger up the steps to the house, lurch against the front door, then pushing it open, walk in. The front door slammed behind him.

I looked up. A curtain covering a second-storey window moved. She was up there, watching . . . the mysterious Mrs. Marshall.

When I got back to Mrs. Hansen's house, I found Olson, Pinner and Tom Mason on the patio.

Mrs. Hansen came out of the living-room as I started up the stairs.

"Oh, Mr. Devery, do come and have a drink. My brother . . ."

I guessed they were burning to know what had happened between Marshall and myself so I joined them on the patio.

I picked up the hostile, suspicious atmosphere as Pinner shoved a chair towards me with his foot. I could understand their attitude. They were thinking: here's a complete stranger who walks into our town and suddenly becomes the favourite of the coming millionaire.

"Seems Frank has taken a liking to you," Pinner said.

I accepted the whisky and soda Olson offered me.

"Drunks are like that," I said. "He tells me he is losing his licence and he can't afford a chauffeur. He wants me to teach his wife to drive."

There was a long pause while the three men absorbed this, then I saw their faces brighten. Maybe this guy, they were probably thinking, wasn't sucking up to the man who they hoped was going to put Wicksteed on the tourist map.

Pinner stroked his moustache.

"Are you going to help out, Keith?"

"That's my job."

A long pause, then he said, "He didn't by chance mention anything about our planning scheme?"

"Not a thing."

The three looked at each other, then Mason said, "He seemed a little hostile when he left with you."

"He was drunk," I said.

"Yes." Olson nodded. "He didn't mean what he said."

Who was kidding who? I thought and finished my drink. I saw no point in sitting around with these three, mulling over Marshall's future.

Getting to my feet, I said I wanted to catch the ball game on TV and would they excuse me?

We shook hands all round and I left them.

Up in my room, I heard them talking. The low rumble of their voices didn't worry me.

Tomorrow I would finally meet Mrs. Beth Marshall.

Beth!

I liked the name.

*　　　*　　　*

As she put the breakfast tray on the table, Mrs. Hansen said, " I brought up the paper. I thought you would like to see it."

I thanked her and had to restrain myself from grabbing it until she had left the room.

The Wicksteed Herald had done a fine snow job on Marshall.

The report, written by the Editor himself, began by giving Marshall a big build up. Quote : *Mr. Marshall is one of our most liked citizens who has always had the interests of Wicksteed close to his heart.* Then, after more blah : *it is common knowledge that Mr. Marshall has been for sometime under considerable strain due to his aunt's distressing illness. His aunt, Mrs. Howard T. Fremlin, has been and will always be our most important citizen. Mr. Marshall frankly admitted that after visiting her at our fine hospital, he was so upset, he took a drink. We think it is unfortunate that Deputy sheriff Ross (a new recruit to our town) felt it necessary to arrest Mr. Marshall when he was about to drive home. Mr. Marshall mistook Deputy sheriff Ross's intentions and pushed him so Deputy sheriff Ross fell against Mr. Marshall's car and slightly injured his mouth. After consulting with his attorney, Mr. Yule Olson, Mr. Marshall agreed that it was only fair that he should lose his driving licence for a few months. Smiling, Mr. Marshall told our reporter: ' It's tough, but there are so many kids around here who drink-drive, I want to set them an example.'*

To me, this was the most vomit making reportage I had ever read. I tossed the paper aside and wondered how Deputy sheriff Ross was reacting.

I had just finished my breakfast when Mrs. Hansen came tapping on my door.

" A telephone call for you, Mr. Devery. It's Mr. Marshall."

I could tell by the way her eyes were popping how excited she was. I went down the stairs and took the call.

" Is that you, Keith?" Marshall's booming voice came over the line.

" How are you, Frank?"

" I could be worse. Listen, I've talked to Beth and she's willing to learn to drive. Is that okay with you?"

" It's my job, Frank."

" Yeah." A pause, then he went on, " Could you come up to the house? She doesn't want to go down to the town. Could you do that?"

To meet Mrs. Beth Marshall, I would have done a moon shot.

" No problem, Frank."

" Well, thanks. Right now I've a taxi waiting to take me to the station. Would eleven o'clock be okay?"

" Why, sure."

" Get her driving fast, Keith. This taxi business is costing me money."

" I'll do my best."

A long pause, then he asked, " Did you see the paper this morning?"

" I saw it."

" Nice job, huh? Elliot—he's the Editor—would kiss my prat if I told him to." He gave a great bellow of laughter. I got the impression that he was a little drunk. " Then you come here at eleven . . . right?"

" I'll be there."

He hung up and I hung up. Then seeing Mrs. Hansen hovering in the living-room, all ears, I told her I was going to Marshall's home to teach Mrs. Marshall to drive.

"That should be very interesting, Mr. Devery," she said, her mouth prim. "You will be the first of us to meet Mrs. Marshall."

"I'll tell you how I find her," I said.

"I'm sure everyone will be interested."

Returning to my room, I put on swim trunks, took a towel and was starting down the stairs when the telephone bell rang.

Mrs. Hansen called to me as I reached the front door.

"Mr. Pinner is asking for you, Mr. Devery."

It seemed I was becoming an important citizen in this one horse town.

"Have you any news from Marshall?" Pinner asked as I picked up the telephone receiver.

I told him Marshall had asked me to give his wife driving lessons.

He grunted, then said, "No one in town has met Mrs. Marshall. We'll be interested to hear what you think of her." A long pause while I imagined he was stroking his moustache. "You remember what I said about her being as important to this town as Frank?"

As if I could have forgotten! I said I remembered.

"Yeah. When will these driving lessons be finished?"

"I wouldn't know. It depends how she makes out."

"That's right." Another pause and probably more moustache stroking. "Well, suppose we get together at Joe's bar at six tonight, huh? I expect Tom will join us and maybe Yule if he can spare the time. Suppose I buy you a drink, Keith?" and he laughed.

"That's fine with me, Mr. Pinner."

"Hey! Cut that mister stuff. I'm Joe to my friends."

"Why, thanks, Joe, I appreciate that." Knowing he couldn't see me, I grinned. "I'll see you at six."

"That's it. We'll be interested to hear what you think of

Mrs. Marshall." His laugh, as sincere as a politician's promise, boomed in my ear. " And Keith, you could probe . . . you know what I mean? It would be constructive from our point of view to find out what she thought of our town and if . . ." He stopped short. It probably occurred to him he was shooting his mouth off too much. " Well, you know, Keith . . . we regard you as one of our friends."

" Thanks, Joe. I know what you mean."

" Fine." If he could have reached down the line and slapped me on the back, he would have done it.

He wasn't fooling me, but I was pretty sure I was fooling him.

*　　*　　*

The clock on the dashboard of my car registered exactly 11.00 as I pulled up outside Frank Marshall's big, lonely house.

I had had a swim. I was wearing a blue sports shirt and white slacks and although looking my best, I wasn't feeling my best. This meeting with the mysterious Mrs. Marshall somehow bothered me. I had a thumping pulse I hadn't before experienced.

Remaining in the car, I looked at the front door, expecting it to open, but it didn't. I waited for some moments, then was forced to the conclusion that Mrs. Beth Marshall wasn't peeping through a curtain. So I got out of the car. Leaving the driving door hanging open, I walked up the steps and thumbed the bell.

Somewhere inside the house, I heard the bell ring. I waited, sweating in the heat, then just as I was about to ring again, the door swung open.

While driving up from Wicksteed, I had tried to imagine what Mrs. Marshall would look like. Hopefully, my first thought was she could be a second Liz Taylor, but I put that image out of my mind, telling myself it would be my bad luck for her to be dumpy, deadly dull and possibly kittenish. After milling over that image, I found it so depressing, I rejected it. At best, I hoped she would be young, pretty and perceptible to male charm : my charm in particular.

The woman who stood in the doorway gave me a jolt of surprise. Around thirty-three, she was almost as tall as myself and she was thin : too thin for my liking. I prefer women with bumps and curves. Her features were good : a long, thin nose, a big mouth and a well sculptured jaw line. Her eyes gave her unusual face its life : black glittering eyes, steady and coldly impersonal. This wasn't a woman with whom you took liberties : strictly no fanny patting.

She was wearing a shapeless dark blue dress that she must have run up herself. I was sure no dress shop would have owned to it. Her black, silky hair, parted in the middle, fell to her shoulders.

During my short stay in Wicksteed, I had had the opportunity to survey some of the female scene. Comparing what I had seen, Mrs. Beth Marshall was a lioness among the roebucks.

" You will be Mr. Devery and you have come to teach me to drive," she said in a quiet, deepish voice.

That took care of the introductions.

" Yes, Mrs. Marshall," I said.

Her black eyes flickered over me, then she walked down the steps and as she passed me, I got a smell of her : a very faint, sexy body smell that was so faint I could have imagined it, but I knew I hadn't.

I remained on the top step and watched her because I wanted to see her walk. The dress, of course, did nothing for her, but it couldn't hide her elegant legs and the hint of an exciting body that moved with confident arrogance. Mrs. Beth Marshall, I decided, would be a hell of a woman when stripped off.

As I started after her, she was already in the driving seat so I went around, opened the off-side door and slid in beside her.

She was looking at the controls.

"Don't tell me," she said curtly. She turned the ignition key and pressed down on the gas pedal. The motor fired. Before I could stop her, she had shifted into drive and the car surged forward. I managed to yank on the handbrake before we hit a tree.

"I should have gone into reverse," she said as if to herself. "I'll try again."

I reached over her, my arm brushing against a small breast. I turned off the motor and removed the ignition key.

"I'm hired to teach you to drive, Mrs. Marshall," I said, turning to look at her. "I'm not here to watch you make dangerous experiments."

"Dangerous experiments?" She continued to examine the controls. "Any idiot can drive . . . look at the idiots who are driving."

"And you are no idiot," I said.

She turned her head slowly and her black, glittering eyes surveyed me. A spooky feeling, like a cold dead finger crept up my spine as we looked at each other.

Leaning forward, she took the ignition key from me.

"I haven't driven for over a year," she said. "Do me a favour, will you, please? Fold your teaching tent, and let me do my thing."

What kind of language is that? I asked myself, but that cold, dead finger still moved up my spine. The car was insured and I could jump out if it came to a crunch and she seemed very sure of herself so I said, "Okay. We can always die together."

This was a joke that wasn't appreciated. She gave me a cold, hostile stare, then started the motor, shifted into reverse, backed out onto the dirt road without knocking down the gatepost, braked, shifted into drive and away we went: a shade too fast for safety, but not so fast as to make my hair ends rise.

At the end of the dirt road that led directly to the highway, she stopped the car and sat staring through the windshield while her long, slim fingers played a muted tune on the steering wheel.

I waited.

Finally, she said in that deep, sexy voice, " I'm not driving into Wicksteed so all those jerks can stare. I haven't been to 'Frisco in years. That's where we'll go."

" Look, Mrs. Marshall," I said, knowing I was wasting my breath. " I think you should have a little more practice . . ."

She could have been deaf. She shifted into drive and we were out onto the highway.

At this hour the traffic was as congested as a kicked over ant hill. I sat still, sweating, as she moved the car into the fast lane. Then, just keeping within the legal speed limit, she held her own with the out-going cowboys.

I said nothing. She said nothing. From time to time, I looked at her. There was a faint, amused smile hovering around her mouth. Although I expected at any moment to shut my eyes, shove my foot through the floorboards, perhaps even scream, I didn't.

Approaching the outskirts of 'Frisco, she moved into the slow lane and leaving the highway, she filtered expertly to a secondary road.

I came to the conclusion that there was nothing I could teach her about handling a car. If her driving had ever been rusty, the rust had now gone.

She seemed to know where she was going which was more than I did. After a ten-minute drive, she slowed and pulled into a parking lot of a restaurant-cum-motel. She drove into a vacant parking bay and stopped, then she turned and regarded me.

" After that experience, Mr. Devery, you could use a drink."

I shook my head.

" The first half hour was scarey, but after that, I enjoyed it. All the same I could use a hamburger or something. Could you?"

She nodded. We got out of the car and walked over to the

restaurant. As we approached the swing door, she said, " I used to work here," then leading the way, she walked into the big, airy restaurant, across to the bar where a short fat man, wearing a chef's hat, was making sandwiches. When he saw her, he stiffened, dropped his knife and his eyes popped wide open.

" For God's sake! Beth!" he exclaimed.

" It's been quite a time, Mario," she said, her voice impersonal. " We were passing. This is Mr. Devery. He is teaching me to drive."

The fat man's eyes swivelled to me and he offered his hand. I shook hands with him.

" Teaching her to drive?" he said blankly.

" She doesn't need much teaching," I said.

He burst into an uneasy laugh.

" You can say that again."

" We're pressed for time, Mario. What's the special for today?" There was a cutting edge to her voice that wiped the smile off Mario's fat face.

" Tenderloin and it's good." His voice had become servile.

She looked at me.

" Okay?"

" Fine."

" Then let's have that, Mario."

" Sure. Pronto. Beers?"

Again she looked at me.

" Fine."

She nodded to him, then walked across to a table away from the bar and sat down. I took the seat opposite her and looked around. It was early, but there were some twenty people already eating. None of them paid us any attention.

" Well, Mr. Devery, do you think I can drive?" she asked.

" Have you a driving licence?"

" I have it."

" Then you don't need lessons from me. You can drive your husband to the station tomorrow."

She opened her handbag and took out a pack of cigarettes. She shook out a cigarette, lit it and blew smoke towards me.

" And suppose I don't want to drive him to the station, Mr. Devery?"

Again the spooky cold dead finger.

" Then, unless you want to make him mad at you, you'll have to have more driving lessons."

She nodded.

" That's what I was hoping you would suggest. That's why I agreed to take lessons."

" He doesn't know you can drive?"

" No."

Mario came over with two plates of food. He set them before us and stood back, looking anxiously at her.

" How's that, Beth?"

She regarded the food, touched her plate and shrugged.

" You don't improve, Mario."

He lifted his hands helplessly.

" The meat's the best."

" That's something. Where's the beer?"

" Pronto."

As he hurried away, I said, " You're a little rough with him, aren't you? This looks good."

" Eat it before the fat congeals."

So we ate.

Mario brought the beers, smirked at me and went away.

She was right. Before we were half-way through, the plates were a mess of white fat. We both pushed them away and both lit cigarettes.

" Some people never learn. I've told him, shown him, yelled at him, but he never will learn that hot plates are as important as good cooking. He'll never learn. Still, we're not poisoned. Coffee?"

" Sure."

She snapped her fingers and Mario, back to cutting sandwiches, nodded.

There was a pause, then he came hurrying over with two cups of coffee. He looked at the half finished meal, grimaced, gathered up the plates and went away.

"That false start you made when you went into drive instead of reverse was an act?" I said as I stirred sugar in my coffee.

She half smiled.

"I like men with quick reactions. You were very quick."

"I earn a living as a driving instructor. I have to be quick."

She studied me for a long moment, her black eyes remote.

"Have you always been an instructor, Mr. Devery?"

"I am what Mr. Olson calls a rolling stone. Do you know Mr. Yule Olson?"

"My husband's attorney. I haven't met him."

We sipped the coffee which was surprisingly good.

"So you once worked here?" I looked around and nodded approval. "Quite a lay out."

"Turn a stone and find a worm." She shrugged. "It's not bad." She flicked ash on the floor. "I met my husband here."

This interested me, but I was careful not to let her see that.

"And you don't want to drive him to the station?"

"No."

"He's lost his driving licence for three months. He has hired me to teach you to drive. Okay, I could give you six or maybe ten driving lessons and if you're not driving by then it will make me look a lousy instructor."

She stubbed out her cigarette.

"I don't think so. It'll make me look an idiot."

"And he knows you are not."

Aware we were embarking on a conspiracy, I felt my pulse rate increase.

"I am not going to drive my drunken husband to the station every morning and I am not picking him up at the station every evening. That's for real!"

Looking at her, I saw her black eyes were glittering.

" Why not tell him driving scares you? I could tell him for you."

She considered this, frowning.

" Yes, that could be a solution, but I wonder . . ." She paused.

" What do you wonder?"

She pushed back her chair and stood up. That sexy body smell came distinctly to me.

" I want to talk to Mario for a few moments. His wife is a good friend of mine. Would you mind waiting, Mr. Devery?"

I watched her walk across to the bar where Mario was polishing glasses. I lit another cigarette.

Her talk with Mario lasted less than five minutes. From time to time I looked at them. She leaned against the bar, her back to me. He stood, a glass in hand, gaping at her. Then she turned away and returned to our table and sat down.

" You were saying, Mrs. Marshall, that you wondered . . ." I said.

She looked directly at me.

" Call me Beth."

My heart skipped a beat.

" What were you wondering, Beth?"

" My husband has no interest in anything except his business and drinking, Keith. I haven't interested him for more than two years." She paused, then went on, " There is a vacant cabin across the way. Mario is understanding." She half smiled, her eyes questioning. " I was wondering . . ."

Right then I should have jumped to my feet, run out to the car and left her, but, of course, I didn't. A surge of lust swamped the red light that began to flash in my mind.

" I don't need to wonder," I said, my voice husky. " What are we waiting for?"

She gave a little nod, stood up and walked to the swing door. As I followed her, I looked at Mario. He was watching, and as I caught his eye, he shook his head in a warning gesture.

Again the red light flashed up and again I ignored it.

I went with her into the hot sunshine and across to the row of cabins. My heart was hammering and I was having trouble with my breathing as she inserted a key into the lock of cabin No. 1 and opened the door.

four

PARKING ON Main street was tight, but I spotted a man about to get into his car a few yards from Joe's saloon. I flicked down my trafficator, braked and stopped. The driver of a car behind me hooted, then passed, giving me a frustrated glare. The parked car moved into the stream of traffic and I manoeuvred into the hole.

As I got out of the car, Deputy sheriff Ross came stalking down the sidewalk. His small cop eyes were bleak, his lips swollen and there was a bruise on his jaw. Marshall had certainly belted him. You don't get those puffed lips from a kiss. We both ignored each other.

Locking the car, I walked over to Joe's saloon.

The reception committee was waiting: Joe Pinner, Yule Olson and Tom Mason. They were sitting at a corner table, away from the bar.

As I joined them the city clock struck six.

" Hi, there, Keith!" Pinner boomed, beaming at me. " What'll you drink?"

The way I was feeling, I needed a treble whisky, but I wanted to continue to create a good impression, so, seeing they were all drinking beer, I said, " A beer would be fine, thanks," and I dropped into a chair beside him. Then looking at the other two, I said, " Gentlemen."

" Hi, Keith," Mason said, nodding and smiling.

More reserved, Olson said, " It is my pleasure, Mr. Devery."

You three stuff shirt hypocrites! I thought as Pinner signalled to Joe. There was a pause while Joe opened a bottle, poured and came over. He set the beer in front of me as he said, " Hi, Mr. Devery."

There were some half dozen men propping up the bar and they were all looking slyly towards us, concentrating on me. I guessed the whole town knew by now that I had met the mysterious Mrs. Beth Marshall.

Unable to contain himself, Pinner said, " Well Keith, how did you find her?"

The three of them leaned forward expectantly.

How did I find her?

I wasn't going to tell them that she was the best lay I had ever had, that I couldn't wait until tomorrow, when we had arranged to meet again, for a repeat performance. I wasn't going to tell them that, as we laid side by side in the cool little motel room, she had told me in that deep sexy voice of hers that the moment she had peered at me through the curtain when I had brought her husband back from the station I had set her on fire. Nor was I going to tell them that there was something about her that spooked me : that sent the feeling of a cold dead finger up my spine even when we were coupled together, and even when we had reached the top of the hill, exploded and slid down into sweating, dazed exhaustion. I wasn't going to tell them any of that.

Instead, I sat back, frowning and appeared to hesitate, then I said, " A bit of a screwball. I guess you could call her an introvert. She scarcely spoke a word." I looked at Pinner with my most beguiling smile. " I tried to make contact . . . nothing so far."

Their faces showed their disappointment.

" So you got no idea how she reacts to our town?" Pinner asked, tugging at his moustache.

I certainly had, but I wasn't going to tell them what she had said about Wicksteed and everyone who lived in the town.

Her scathing comments had even surprised me.

"The opportunity didn't come up," I lied. I drank some beer, then went on, "But it could . . ." and let it hang.

The three sat forward.

"Is that a fact?" Mason asked.

Glancing over my shoulder, I shifted my chair forward, then lowering my voice, I said, "Strictly in confidence, I doubt if Mrs. Marshall will ever learn to drive. Some women are too scared to drive. Some women haven't the concentration to drive. Some women have a blind spot when at the wheel of a car. From what I've seen of Mrs. Marshall's efforts so far, I'd say the chances of her passing the test is more than remote."

The three looked at each other.

Olson said, "So what is the position, Mr. Devery?"

"I've been worrying about it, Mr. Olson. I want to be helpful. I realise how important it is to you to know how she reacts to Wicksteed." I paused and looked at the three of them, then went on, "It seems to me there are two alternatives."

Pinner said sharply, "And what are they?"

"Well, I guess the honest thing to do is to tell Marshall that his wife is not capable of passing the test and so save him the cost of further lessons. If I tell him that I lose contact with Mrs. Marshall and I won't be able to get the information you want." I paused to let that sink in, then went on, "The other alternative is for me to go on giving her lessons and hope she will unwind."

Olson said, frowning, "Unwind? What does that mean?"

"I mean for her to relax. Once she relaxes, I could ask her how she reacts to Wicksteed. I might even persuade her to confide in me about her future plans if her husband died." I looked straight at Pinner. "That's the information you want, isn't it?"

Pinner tugged at his moustache as he nodded.

"That's what we want, Keith," he said. "You go on giving her driving lessons. You do that."

Olson shifted uneasily.

" Just a moment. If Mr. Devery is so certain she won't be able to drive . . ." He paused and looked at Mason. " I'm not sure I approve of this. Frank is my client. If Mr. Devery is satisfied that Mrs. Marshall can't pass the test, I think Frank should be told."

Before Mason could express an opinion, I said, " Fine. I was only trying to be helpful. Okay, Mr. Olson, as soon as Frank gets home tonight I'll telephone him and tell him how it is."

" Now wait a minute," Mason said hastily. " Don't let us rush this. We want to know Mrs. Marshall's attitude to our town. Let me ask you a question, Keith. Are you absolutely certain that Mrs. Marshall won't pass the test?"

I nearly laughed. This was exactly what I was hoping he would say.

" Can anyone be absolutely certain of anything. No . . . she just might, but I doubt it."

" So why don't you give her a few more lessons and while you are with her, ask a few questions?" Mason asked. " How's about that?"

I looked at Olson.

" I'm only too happy to help. You tell me what you want, and I'll do it."

Pinner slapped his hand down on the table, making the glasses jump.

" Tom's got the solution!"

Olson hesitated, then nodded.

" There can be no harm in giving her a few more lessons. Yes, why not?"

Mason put his hand on my arm.

" You go ahead, Keith. Suppose we all meet here Friday evening. That'll give you three days. Then, if you are sure she won't be able to drive, you tell Frank." He smiled at me, knowingly. " But in the meantime, try to get the information we want."

" You can rely on me, gentlemen." I finished my beer. " So here Friday at six."

" That's it," Pinner said.

" This is supposed to be my day off." I got to my feet. " I'm taking a swim if you'll excuse me." I smiled at them. " Friday then." We shook hands all round, then waving to Joe at the bar, I walked out to my car.

The last thing I wanted was a swim. All I longed to do was to flop on my bed and hope my body would come together again.

Making love to Beth was like getting entangled in a cement mixer.

*　　*　　*

The following morning, still feeling rough, I arrived at the Driving school at 09.00 to be told by Maisie that I was booked solid for one hour driving lessons until 15.00.

I told Bert that I had spent half my day off giving Mrs. Marshall her first driving lesson. I could have saved my breath. He already knew. The grape-vine in this town was fierce.

" That was mighty good of you, Keith," he said. " It's good business. We can charge Marshall double time with you going up to his house and back." He looked inquiringly at me. " How does she shape?"

I didn't tell him that her shape, when stripped off, was sensational. Instead, I said it was early days, but she didn't shape up too well.

" Never mind. It's good money." He began to open his mail. " Did you think any more about my proposition, Keith?"

Proposition? I stared at him blankly, then remembered he had offered me a partnership.

" Not yet, Bert. What with one thing and another . . ."

He looked sad, then shrugged.

" There's time. I just hoped you would have thought about it."

" I'm sorry, Bert. I will."

" Tom will be back tomorrow."

Tom?

I pulled myself together. Marshall and his money plus Beth had blotted everything else from my mind.

Tom Lucas, I now remembered, was Bert's driving instructor before I had arrived on the scene.

" So he is coming back?"

" That's it, Keith. He's okay now and he'll ease the pressure."

Maisie looked in to tell me my first pupil was waiting.

Although I kept busy, the morning dragged. At lunch time, I went to a call booth, found Marshall's home number and dialled.

Her deep, sexy voice gave me that spooky feeling as she said, " This is Mrs. Marshall speaking."

" I can't be with you until five. When will he be back?"

" He is staying the night at 'Frisco." A pause, then she said, " Do you want to spend the night with me?"

Did I want to? Did I want to grab Marshall's million dollar inheritance? But the red light flashed up and this time I paid attention.

" Let's talk about it, Beth," and I hung up.

As I walked across to Joe's saloon for a sandwich and a Coke, I decided that, much as I wanted to spend the night with Beth, it was too dangerous. How would I explain to Mrs. Hansen that I wasn't sleeping this night in my room? I had already had a session with her, telling her that Mrs. Beth Marshall seemed a little odd, that she was unfriendly and that she scarcely said a word. Obviously disappointed, Mrs. Hansen had shaken her head as she said, " I don't like the sound of her."

Reluctantly, I decided I couldn't spend the night with Beth. The grape-vine was too fierce. It would have to be a quick screw and then *au revoir*.

Around 16.45, I drove up the dirt road and into Marshall's

garage. I closed the garage doors, then walked up the steps and as I was about to thumb the bell, the front door jerked open.

She was ready for action. She was naked under the see-through white wrap. Catching hold of my wrist, she pulled me up the broad stairway and into a bedroom : probably a guest room. Her fingers were already unbuttoning my shirt as I kicked the door shut.

It was a repeat performance. Only this time, she was at home. She had no inhibitions. When we reached the top of the hill, she gave a wild cry that echoed through the still, lonely house.

This time, the slide down the hill was slower, but the feeling of being fed through a cement mixer remained.

We dozed the way satiated lovers always doze. The room was cool, the light dim. The rustle of leaves in the breeze was the only sound to come through the open window.

After a while we surfaced. I found my pack of cigarettes, gave her one, took one myself and lit up for both of us.

" You're a marvellous lover," she said drowsily.

" You are the best ever."

Lying on the bed, inhaling smoke, my eyes closed, I wondered how many times these banal words had been said by other lovers.

" Will you stay the night, Keith ?"

That was what I wanted to do. She had thrown a hook in me. Sexually, she was the most exciting woman I had ever known, and, in the past I had known a lot of women. She had now such a hook in me that I hesitated before saying, " No. I want to, Beth, but it's too dangerous. You may not know it, but the whole goddamn town is watching me. I am the first to contact you . . . you who are the second most important person to them. Everyone is watching me. Did you know that ?"

She moved her long body on the crumpled sheet.

" I could be the first most important person, not the second most important person," she said so quietly I scarcely heard her, but I did.

I looked at her.

She lay there, naked, a cigarette between her long, slim fingers, her eyes closed, her face as expressionless as a death mask.

" Say that again." I raised myself up and looked down at her.

" Nothing." She must have known I was leaning over her, but her eyes remained closed. " Women talk . . . nothing."

She moved her hand. Hot ash fell on my chest.

" When am I seeing you again, Keith?"

I brushed off the ash.

" Do you know he is going to be worth a million dollars when his aunt dies?"

She moved her long legs, opening them, then bringing them together.

" Know? Why else do you imagine I married him?"

I thought of Marshall: fat, a drunk and then looking at her: lean, long: a lioness.

" Yes. There could be no other reason."

" And you?" She half turned her head so she could look at me, her black eyes remote. " You are interested in his money, aren't you, Keith?"

This startled me, but I kept my face expressionless as I said, " I am interested in money . . . any money."

She gave a malicious little laugh.

" Well, he hasn't got it yet. So no one, including you and including me, need get interested."

" That's where you're wrong." I told her about the Planning committee and how I had become involved and that I was playing along with them and that I was seeing them on Friday evening.

She listened while she stared up at the ceiling.

" By playing along with them," I went on, " it gives me a legitimate excuse to be with you if we are seen together. There are eyes everywhere, Beth."

" Hmmm." She stretched her long legs. " You can tell them Frank won't give them a cent. He hates Wicksteed. If he died, I wouldn't give them a cent either."

" I won't tell them that. That's not the way to handle it if we're going to go on seeing each other."

She shrugged her naked shoulders.

" Tell them what you like, but you now know not one cent of old Mrs. Fremlin's money will ever be spent on this stinking little town . . . that's for real : neither by Frank nor by me."

She rolled over to stub out her cigarette. She had a long, lean beautiful back right down to the cleft of her buttocks.

" Keith . . . don't underestimate Frank. No one . . . repeat no one . . . will get anything from him. He may be a drunk, but he still remains smart. Don't make any plans."

I stiffened, staring at her.

" Plans ?"

She didn't look at me. Her eyes were half closed, her lips parted in a half smile.

" I'm not with you, Beth. What do you mean . . . plans?"

" There isn't one man nor one woman in Wicksteed who isn't hoping to grab some of the money when that old woman dies." Her smile twisted cynically. " And you are no exception."

" And neither are you," I said.

Again the malicious little laugh.

" I'll get the lot anyway . . . if he dies. He is years older than I am and he is drinking himself to death. I can wait."

" Are you sure he is leaving the money to you?"

She nodded.

" I'm sure. I have seen his will."

" He could change his mind."

" Not now . . . his mind isn't capable of changing."

" What do you mean ?"

" He drinks. He has set ideas. He's made a will. I've seen it. He won't be bothered to make another. Why should he care anyway? He can't use the money when he's dead."

"What would you do if he died and you got all this money?"

She drew in a long slow breath. Her hands moved over her tiny breasts and caressed them.

"Do? I would go back to 'Frisco where I was born. A woman with a million dollars can have a ball in 'Frisco."

"Alone?"

She looked at me, her black eyes suddenly glittering and she dropped her hand on mine.

"You are never alone with a million dollars, but would you want to come along?"

Would I want to?

"I would want to come along, Beth, without the million dollars."

Her fingers tightened on mine.

"That's a pretty speech." She smiled at me, her eyes remote again. "But, Keith, no man on earth could take me away from Frank while he is alive."

Somewhere below, a clock struck six.

I remembered where I was and that I had a half hour drive back to Wicksteed.

"I must go. If I'm late for dinner, there will be gossip." I swung off the bed and began to dress. "The same time tomorrow?"

"Hmmm."

We looked at each other, then I bent and kissed her. Her lips felt dry and they didn't move under mine.

"Then tomorrow . . ."

As I reached the door, she said quietly, "Keith . . ."

I paused and looked at her, lying flat on her back, naked, her long legs tightly together, her black silky hair spread on the pillow, her lips parted in a strange little smile.

"Go on," I said.

"Don't make any plans without me."

I stared at her, again feeling that spooky feeling.

"Plans?"

" You know. You want his money and so do I." She lifted her hair and resettled it on the pillow. " Both of us, Keith . . . both of us together."

The clock chimed the quarter hour.

" We'll talk about it tomorrow," I said.

Leaving her, I walked down the stairway and to my car. As I drove down the dirt road, I thought of what she had said.

There was something about her that made me uneasy. There was something fatal about her. Fatal? An odd word, but the only word that seemed to fit her.

How had she guessed? Intuition?

You want his money.

Then she had said : " Don't underestimate Frank. No one . . . repeat no one . . . is going to get the money when he gets it."

A warning?

Then she had said : " Don't make any plans without me."

Unless I was reading her wrong, and I was sure I wasn't, this was a plain invitation to join her in some plan to get his money.

As I edged into the traffic on the highway, I decided I would have to play it by ear. I had time, I told myself. The old lady was still alive. Tomorrow, I would talk again to Beth and there must be no more hints, no more hedging.

Leaving the car in Mrs. Hansen's garage, I walked into the hall and started up the stairs to my room. Mrs. Hansen came out of the living-room, a handkerchief in her hands, her eyes red from crying.

" Oh, Mr. Devery, I do apologise . . . your dinner will be late."

I paused, staring at her.

" That's okay, Mrs. Hansen. Has something happened?"

" My dear friend . . . Mrs. Fremlin . . . passed away an hour ago."

My heart skipped a beat, then began to race. Somehow, I forced the right expression on my face.

" I'm so sorry."

" Thank you, Mr. Devery. It was inevitable, but it is still a great shock and a great loss to me."

I said all the things one should say on such an occasion. I said not to bother about dinner. I would eat out. I even patted her shoulder.

As I walked back to the garage, all I could think of was that Marshall was now a millionaire and the time I had thought I had now had run out.

On the way down town, I stopped off at a call booth.

" She's dead," I said when Beth came on the line.

I heard her catch her breath.

" Say that again !"

" She died an hour ago. It'll be all over the town by now."

" At last !" The note of triumph in her voice gave me that spooky feeling again.

" You are now the wife of a millionaire," I said.

She didn't reply, but I could hear her quick breathing over the line.

" I must talk to you, Beth . . . about plans. I'll come up tonight when it is dark."

She reacted immediately.

" No ! As soon as he knows, he'll be back. He's probably on his way now. No, you must keep away from me !"

Standing in the hot call booth, I suddenly realised that there would be no more driving lessons. Marshall could afford a chauffeur. There would be no more rolling in the hay with Beth. Marshall would give up his real estate business in 'Frisco and do his drinking at home.

" When do we meet, Beth ?" I asked, suddenly anxious.

" I don't know." Her voice sounded remote. " I'll arrange something. Keep away. I'll call you."

" Now listen, Beth, this is important. We've got to meet somewhere and soon. We . . ." I stopped talking, realising she had hung up.

Slowly, I replaced the receiver, pushed open the booth door and walked back to my car.

This woman had really thrown a hook in me. As I sat in the car, staring through the dusty windshield, I realised that even if she hadn't been the wife of a millionaire, even if she had been working in a restaurant, I would still want her. Closing my eyes, I could hear her wild cry as she had reached the top of the hill. No woman I had ever been with had reacted to my thrusts as she had and this truly hooked me. Now this sudden bleak outlook. It had, of course been too easy. I had stupidly imagined that I could drive up to that house every day with the pretext of teaching her to drive but instead, get her on the bed.

Well, she had said she would arrange something. I would have to wait. I had always been patient, but waiting for Beth was something else beside.

I started the motor and drove towards Wicksteed.

*   *   *

I returned to my room soon after 21.00. To avoid running into any of the Planning committee, I had eaten at a cheap restaurant off Main street, but even there, everyone was talking about Mrs. Fremlin's death.

I sat at a corner table and chewed through a tough steak and listened.

The conversation floated around me.

I bet old Frank will drink himself to death now he's getting all that money.

It wouldn't surprise me now he's collecting that money that he left Wicksteed.

Joe Pinner has great hopes that Frank will put up some money. The amusement park idea is great. We'll all benefit. and so on and so on.

A newcomer came in : a big, fat man, shabbily dressed, who joined the other six men at a table near mine.

"I've just seen Frank," he said. "Just came off the train. He's drunker than a skunk." He gave a bellow of laughter. "Tom Mason was there and drove him home. Tom's no fool. He has his eye on Frank's money."

And he's not the only one, I thought, paid my check and went out to my car.

Groups of people were standing around, talking. There was only one topic of conversation in Wicksteed this night.

Back in my room, I turned on the TV set and sat down. After three or four minutes, I got up, turned the set off and began to prowl around the room.

I had Beth on my mind.

Lust for her moved through me like a knife thrust.

When was I going to see her again?

She was in my blood now like a virus. *I'll arrange something.* But what? How long would I have to wait? I thought of Marshall. Several times while Beth had talked she had said: *when he dies: if he dies: when he is dead.*

With Marshall out of the way, she would have his money. *Don't make any plans without me, Keith.*

Lighting a cigarette, I continued to prowl around the room. Death, I thought, solved so many problems. If Marshall died . . .

I paused to stare out at the moonlit beach.

I couldn't walk up to him, tap him on his fat chest and say, "Do me a favour—drop dead." I couldn't do that, but that was now my thinking. If he did drop dead, it would be more than a favour. I could have Beth and also his money.

A gentle tapping on my door snapped me out of this thinking. I opened up.

Mrs. Hansen said, "You are wanted on the telephone, Mr. Devery. It's Mr. Marshall."

I stared at her, feeling spooked.

"Mr. Marshall?"

She nodded. Her eyes bright with excitement.

"Thank you."

I moved by her and went down the stairs.

" Is that you, Keith?" There was no mistaking Marshall's booming voice. " Have you heard the news?"

" Who hasn't? My condolences and my congratulations."

He laughed. I could tell by his laugh, he was pretty drunk.

" It comes to us all, and it wasn't too soon. Listen, Keith, suppose you come up here? I want to talk to you."

This was so unexpected, I stared blankly at the wall for a long moment, then I said, " You mean right now?"

" Why not? Let's make a night of it. How's about it?"

" Fine . . . I'm on my way."

" I mean a night of it, Keith. Bring a toothbrush. We've plenty of spare beds," and he hung up.

Aware Mrs. Hansen was still hovering, I said, " He sounds a little drunk. He's asking me to spend the night with him."

Not giving her a chance to comment, I went up to my room, threw my shaving and wash kit into a hold-all, added a clean shirt and pyjamas and then hurried down to the hall.

Mrs. Hansen was still hovering. I waved to her, knowing for sure, the moment she heard my car drive away, she would be on the telephone to her brother, spreading the news.

I had this feeling of fatality which I had had ever since I had met Beth. I now accepted the fact that she meant more to me than money. And now, for no reason I could think of, Marshall had invited me to spend the night in their house. Why? Again fatality?

Parking the car outside the house, I thumbed the bell push. Lights were on in the living-room. As I stood in the moonlight, my heart beating unevenly, I heard heavy footfalls. The door jerked open and Marshall stood there, his fat, red, smiling face shiny with sweat.

" Come on in and join the Big shot," he said, lurched a little, grabbed hold of my arm and led me into the living-room.

I looked quickly around. There was no sign of Beth.

" Have a drink." He waved to a half empty bottle of Scotch. " There's plenty more." Lurching by me, he poured a big drink, slopped in charge water, then thrust the glass into my hand. He then lurched to an armchair and collapsed into it. "I guess I've tied one on, Keith," he said. "Who wouldn't? A million dollars! At last! Something to celebrate, huh?"

I sat opposite him.

"Congratulations, Frank."

He squinted at me.

"Yeah." He paused, screwing up his eyes, then went on, "You know something, Keith? I like you. You are my people. You're not like these creeps who are after my money. I like you." He blew out his cheeks. "Don't pay too much attention to what I'm saying . . . I guess I'm drunk, but I'm telling you for a fact, I like you."

"Thanks, Frank," I said. "People meet . . . people take to each other. It happens."

He peered drunkenly at me.

"Do you like me, Keith?" There was a pleading, unhappy note in his voice.

Do me a favour . . . drop dead.

But I wasn't going to say that to him. Instead, I lifted my glass in a salute.

"You are my people too, Frank."

"Yeah." He nodded. "I felt it. When you drove me back here and then walked all that way back, I told myself you were my people."

I wondered how much longer this stupid, drunken talk could continue. I wondered where Beth was.

"Coming back in the train, Keith, I got thinking," he went on. "I'm going to be busy. I've got to wind up my estate business. I've got all kinds of plans." He rubbed his hand over his sweating face and peered at me. "Tell me something . . . how did you get on with my wife . . . with Beth?"

This was so unexpected, I sat still, staring at him.

"Huh?" He frowned, trying to focus me. "How did you get on with her?"

"Fine." My voice was husky, "but she isn't easy to teach."

He laughed : his great bellowing laugh.

" Between you and me, Keith, she is conning you. I know she can handle a car as well as you can, but she doesn't want to drive me." He lifted his heavy shoulders in a shrug. " I don't blame her. I'm a drunk. These creeps in this town stare and yak." He closed his eyes, shook his head, opened his eyes as he said, " She is a very special woman, Keith. That's why I married her." He blew out his cheeks, then went on, " I met her at a restaurant off the 'Frisco highway. I went in there for lunch and there she was. She hooked me. There was that something about her . . ." He shook his head. " Something very special. I've screwed around in my day, but this woman . . . something very special, Keith."

As if I didn't know. I just sat there, listening.

" I went in there every day for a week and the more I saw her the more I got hooked. She seemed to like me and when she told me she had had enough of the restaurant, it was my chance. So we got married. Then I found out she was a real loner." He grimaced. " Well, we all have our kinks. I don't give a damn. She runs the house, cooks well, looks after the garden . . . so why the hell should I care?" He pointed a shaking finger at me. " She's reliable, Keith. That's what I like about her. I know when I get back from work, she'll have a good dinner for me. I know I'll get a clean shirt when I want one. I know there'll always be whisky in the house . . . that's what she is . . . reliable."

I continued to listen, watching him as he picked up his glass, stared at it, then finished the drink.

" Now what was I saying?" He frowned, shook his head, then peered at me. " Yeah. I was telling you . . . coming back in the train, I got thinking." He held out his glass. " Let's have another, Keith."

I got up, took his glass and fixed him a whisky and soda that would have knocked out a mule.

" Thanks." He took the glass, drank, sighed, nodded, then went on, " How much is Ryder paying you?"

"Two hundred."

"That's not much. Look, Keith, I'm going to be busy. I can't drive a car. I want someone to take me around." He leaned forward. "I thought of you. How would you like to be my chauffeur? How's about it?"

Again this was so unexpected, I just sat there, staring at him.

He waved his glass at me, grinning.

"How do you like the idea?"

I drew in a long, slow breath.

"Just what would you want me to do, Frank?"

He nodded approvingly.

"That's a good question. You would have to live here, take me to the railroad station, meet me, take me around and maybe help around in the house." He raised his hand. "Now don't think this is a pissy little job I'm offering you. Okay, maybe it looks like it, but it is only until I get the money and get my driving licence back. I'm asking you to help out until I'm fixed. As soon as I get the money, Keith, I'm getting out of this god-awful town. I'm planning to buy a house in Carmel. Have you ever been to Carmel? It's a great little place. I've got my eye on a house that is coming into the market: really something with ten acres, a big swimming pool, you name it, it's got it. Beth won't be able to handle it, but you can. I would want you to handle the staff, look after the entertaining." He belched, shook his head, took a drink, then went on, "Money makes money. A guy worth a million bucks has to circulate. Now look, Keith, I'll pay you right now seven hundred against Ryder's two hundred, but when I'm fixed, you'll get a damn sight more. What do you say? How's about it?"

You would have to live here . . . maybe help around the house.

My heart began to race. If I took him up on this, I would be right next to Beth and that was what I wanted, but I warned myself not to appear too eager. I mustn't let him suspect what Beth meant to me.

" I appreciate this, Frank," I said, " but Ryder wants me to be his partner. I've been considering his offer. He wants me to have his business when he retires."

Marshall squinted at me.

" A one horse business in a one horse town. Use your head, Keith. You throw in with me and you'll be hitching your wagon to a star. Okay, you start small with me, but you'll grow as I am going to grow. Do you know anything about accountancy?"

For a long moment I hesitated, then I said, " Before I was drafted into the army, Frank, I worked with Barton Sharman."

He gaped at me.

" You mean the stockbrokers?"

" Correct."

" You worked with them?"

" I handled fifteen per cent of their most important clients."

His bleary eyes narrowed.

" Well, for God's sake . . . what are you doing teaching creeps to drive?"

" That's a good question." I smiled at him, my hands moist, my heart thumping. " Vietnam unsettled me. I spent two years killing Viets and sweating it out in the jungle. When I returned to my desk, I couldn't settle. I found money didn't mean much to me. I got the urge to go footloose . . . so I went footloose. It's as simple as that."

He brooded for so long I thought he had fallen asleep.

Finally, he came to the surface and said, " I could use your brains, Keith. Come on . . . forget Ryder. Seven hundred to start and we work together . . . how's about it?"

I could see the drink I had made him was the finaliser.

" Suppose we talk about it tomorrow, Frank?"

" Huh?"

" Let's talk about it tomorrow."

" Yeah. A good idea." He shook his head. " I don't seem able to keep my goddamn eyes open." He heaved himself to his feet. " Come on. Let's go to bed."

He lurched out of the room and up the stairs. He paused outside the room in which Beth and I had made love.

"That's yours. We'll talk tomorrow." Moving slowly and heavily, he walked to the end of the corridor, opened a door, turned on the light, went in and closed the door.

I stood in the corridor, my hand on the door knob and wondered where Beth was. My lust for her raged through me, but, I told myself, it would be asking for trouble to tap on doors, trying to find her. Drunk as he was, Marshall might not be drunk enough.

I walked into the room and snapped on the light.

She was lying on the bed, her hands behind her head, her white see-through wrap scarcely concealing her nakedness.

We looked at each other, then I shut the door and turned the key in the lock.

five

THE CLOCK below stairs woke me as it began to chime seven. The sun was coming through the open window, making a hot patch on the big bed. For some moments, I lay there, feeling utterly drained, then remembering, I looked to my right where she had lain, but she had gone. I threw off the sheet and groped for a cigarette.

When I had joined her on the bed last night, my hands reaching for her, she had said sharply, " No . . . not yet. I was listening. What are you going to do, Keith? Are you going to accept his offer?"

" What do you think?"

We spoke in whispers.

" You'd be a fool if you didn't."

" And I'm no fool."

That malicious little smile lit up her face.

" But remember, Keith, don't underestimate him. He's no fool either."

" You told me," and my hand dropped on her flat belly and moved further down.

End of the conversation.

During that wild night we came together three times. Each time when we reached the top of the hill, she rammed her mouth against my neck to cut off her wild cry. Both of us were very aware that Marshall was sleeping not thirty yards away.

Now, lying on the bed, the cigarette smouldering between my fingers, I reviewed the situation. It looked good to me. I had dropped into a situation I hadn't thought possible. I was inside the fort whereas all those creeps in Wicksteed, thirsting to get their fingers on some of Marshall's money, were strictly on the outside. Now, I told myself, I would have to play my cards carefully. She had twice warned me not to underestimate this fat drunk. Well, okay, I was warned. So first I must probe. I wanted to satisfy myself she knew what she was saying and I hoped she didn't.

I spent the next half hour thinking about the situation, then I heaved myself off the bed and went along the corridor to the bathroom. Showered and shaved, I returned to the bedroom and dressed, then I went down and into the living-room.

The smell of grilling bacon reminded me I was hungry. I walked into the kitchen.

Beth was by the stove, the grill on, the bacon spitting, eggs in the frypan.

We looked at each other and she gave me her remote smile.

" Did you sleep well, Mr. Devery?" The red light was on.

" Fine, thank you. That smells good."

" How do you like your eggs?"

" As they come."

She had such a hook in me that I longed to grab her and let my hands slide down that long, beautiful back until I cupped her buttocks, but her remote eyes warned me off.

" Hi, Keith!"

Startled, I turned.

Marshall was standing in the kitchen doorway. Considering the state he had been in the previous night, he looked pretty good. He laid a heavy hand on my arm.

" While we eat, let's talk." He beamed at Beth. " Ready soon?"

" Coming up."

I went with him into the dining-room. The table was laid, coffee in a percolator was ready. There was toast and as we sat down, she came in and put plates of eggs and bacon before us.

"I told you," he said, grinning at me. "Look at this! My wife's reliable."

I didn't say anything.

"I have a job to do in the garden, Frank," she said in her deep, sexy voice. "Enjoy your breakfast," and she went away.

"She never stops working in the garden," he said, pouring coffee. "Well, Keith, are you throwing in with me?"

"I'd be stupid if I didn't, wouldn't I?"

He regarded me, then began spreading butter on his toast. "That's for sure. Okay. I want you to drive me to the station. I've got business in 'Frisco this morning, but I'll be back on the 12.30 express. Meet me. We'll have lunch and then I've got to talk to Olson."

"Okay, and I'll have to talk to Ryder."

He dismissed this with an airy wave of his hand. He was already acting as a millionaire.

"You have all the morning."

I began my probe.

"An idea struck me this morning, Frank," I said. "Would you be interested in buying Ryder out? From what I've seen of his business, it's sound and could make you a decent profit. If you like the idea, I could get figures and we could talk about it tonight."

He shovelled eggs and bacon into his mouth.

"Not interested. Now, listen, Keith, I'm going big. Ryder's pissy little business doesn't interest me."

I nodded.

"Then there's another proposition, Frank. The Planning committee . . ."

"You heard about that?" He grinned. "Their pissy amusement park? They can shove that. I don't want anything to do with Wicksteed . . . that's strictly out."

Don't underestimate him.

"I just thought you might be interested."

" Sure. I want you to feed me ideas, but Wicksteed is out."

" Well, it's your money, Frank." I paused to sip my coffee, then went on, " This amusement park could turn into a hell of a good investment. I've swung deals like this before when I was with Barton Sharman."

" Okay, so it could be a hell of a little investment, but I'm not interested." He bit into his toast. " I've been around, Keith. Real estate is my business. I know what a million dollars can produce. Repeat . . . I don't want anything to do with Wicksteed."

As she had said, he was going to be difficult to handle. Again the thought came into my mind: *Do me a favour . . . drop dead.*

" You're the boss, Frank."

" That's it." He shoved back his chair. " Let's get going. I've a hell of a day ahead."

Without seeing Beth again, I drove him to the station, then I drove to the Driving school. Although it was only 8.45, Bert was already at his desk.

I explained the situation. I said Marshall wanted me to be his chauffeur and he was offering me seven hundred and wanted me to grow with him. I put the cards on the table because I liked Bert and didn't want to play tricky.

" Bert, you know my situation. Frank knows about it (a lie) and this is a chance I should take."

He looked at me, his eyes showing his disappointment.

" I understand, Keith. Well . . ." He lifted his hands. " Tom will handle the driving lessons. I guess I won't retire now for a while." He shook his head. " We all have to plough our own furrow. If that's what you want, I understand."

" I told you, Bert, I'm footloose."

He nodded and that was that.

Maisie shook my hand and Tom Lucas patted my shoulder. I was half sorry to quit : these were decent people.

As I started towards the car, I suddenly realised it was no longer mine to use. I was standing there, wondering what to do when Tom Mason pulled up in his dusty Ford.

" Hi, Keith! You look as if you have a problem."

I walked over and leaned against his car.

" No problem, Tom. How are you?"

" Me? I can't grumble. Do you want to go some place?"

" Not right now." I went around and slid into the passenger's seat, ". but I want a word with you."

" Say on." He looked inquiringly at me.

I gave it to him straight. I told him Marshall had hired me to be his chauffeur, that as soon as he got his inheritance, he planned to quit Wicksteed, that I had suggested he could do a lot worse than to invest some of his money in the amusement park and how he had reacted.

" So there it is, Tom," I concluded. " Maybe I can do something later . . . talk sense into him, but right now, it looks bad."

His face expressed his disappointment.

" But would you want to be his chauffeur, Keith? I understand that Bert has offered you a partnership."

" That's right, but I'm footloose. I'll go along with Marshall for a while. It could be interesting." I opened the car door. " I wanted you to know. Tell Joe and Mr. Olson."

I left him and walked down the street to the cab rank, aware everyone on the street was watching me. I told the cabby to drive me back to Marshall's home.

Beth was in the garden, cutting roses as the cab pulled up. I paid off the cabby and waited in the hot sun until he had driven away. By this time she had gone into the house.

I found her stripping off in my bedroom. I was out of my clothes as she dropped across the bed.

We grabbed each other and her wild cry ran through the silent house.

* * *

I parked Marshall's Plymouth in the station yard a few

minutes to 12.30. He hadn't bothered to get the car fixed since he had had the accident. It had a crumpled wing and a smashed headlight, but it still ran.

As I was getting out of the car, Deputy sheriff Ross materialised. He surveyed the car, then looked me over, his little cop's eyes bleak, his mouth still puffy.

" That's not fit to be on the road," he said, pointing to the bust wing.

" You take it up with Mr. Marshall, this town's millionaire," I said. " I'm just the hired hand," and moving around him, I walked up the slope to the railroad station.

" Hey, Mac ! "

I paused, turned and stared at him.

" Lay off me, Ross," I said quietly, " or if you want to make something of it, we'll go to the cop house and talk to McQueen."

" I'm reporting this car," he said, then putting his thumbs into his gun belt, he stalked away.

The 'Frisco express was pulling in as I reached the platform. Marshall was one of the first to get off. His face was flushed, but he seemed sober enough.

" Hi, Keith ! " He threw his arm around my shoulders. " It's been a heavy morning. Okay with you ? "

" Fine." My mind switched to Beth. " All fixed."

" Let's eat." He came out into the sunshine and walked over to the Plymouth.

" Frank . . . I've had Deputy sheriff Ross on my tail. He says this car isn't road worthy and he's putting in a report."

Marshall regarded the car and grimaced, nodded and dropped into the passenger's seat. There were some twenty to thirty people coming out of the station and they were all trying to catch his eye, smiling and waving at him, but he ignored them.

As I drove off, he said, " Get another car, Keith. Something top class. I'll leave it to you. I've got credit now. The sky is the roof."

"Don't you want to handle it, Frank? Buying a car is important."

"I'm busy." He scowled. "Let's eat. We'll go to the Lobster Grill."

I had heard of this restaurant . . . the best in town.

It took us only five minutes to reach the restaurant and only two minutes to be bowed to a corner table. The grape-vine was working. The Maitre d' and all the waiters showed they were dealing with millionaire material. Marshall loved it.

We ate our way through a complicated dish of lobsters and sole. He didn't talk, but kept frowning as he shovelled the food into his face. I could see he was far away in his thoughts and probably didn't even know what he was eating.

When we were through, he shoved aside his plate, then looking at his watch, he said, " I've got a date with that creep Olson. You go buy a car, Keith."

"But what kind of car?"

He got to his feet, settled the check, then started to the door.

" Buy something right. I'll leave it to you. A status symbol."

So I drove him to Olson's office, left him there and then drove to the Cadillac showroom.

When I said I was buying on behalf of Mr. Frank Marshall, the salesmen practically got down on their knees.

They said they had something very special: a hand built job that had just come onto the market. It was a sleek drop-head in cream and blue with every gimmick a car builder could dream up. They were so anxious to sell it, they didn't even ask me to sign anything. I screwed them for the Plymouth, told them to contact Mr. Marshall for payment, then getting into this beauty, I floated her out onto Main street and that caused a sensation.

I was sitting in her, listening to the stereo radio when I saw Marshall come out of Olson's office. I tapped the horn. It gave off a soft, melodious sound, then I waved to him.

He came swaggering across the sidewalk while people stared. He paused, then walked slowly around the car while I held the passenger's door open. He went around the car three times. He practically stopped the traffic. Everyone now was staring and cars drew to the kerb so the drivers could also stare.

On his third walk around, I said, " Is it okay, Frank? We can get rid of it if you hate it."

He gave his great bellowing laugh.

" Keith! You're my people! This is my car! Where the hell did you find it?"

Aware that there was now quite a crowd staring, I eased him into the passenger's seat, shut the door, ran around and slid under the driving wheel.

" You asked for a car . . . you've got it." I started the motor, turned up the stereo radio and drifted away, leaving the crowd gaping after us.

" Jesus!" he exclaimed. " This is a car!"

I touched the gas pedal and the car surged forward with all the power that eight cylinders can give out, then I throttled back. I was having as big a ball as he was.

" What did it cost, Keith?"

I told him.

" Chick feed." He blew out his cheeks. " A million dollars! Goddamn it . . . I could buy ten of these cars if I wanted to."

" But you don't."

" That's right." He rubbed his hand over his face. " I could do with a drink."

As if I hadn't thought of that. I opened the glove compartment and took out a half of Scotch and handed it to him. He clamped the bottle to his mouth and drank the way a baby sucks milk.

He had killed the bottle by the time I had reached the house. There was no sign of Beth. I helped him out of the car. He lurched up the steps and I watched him enter the house, then I drove the car into the garage. I sat for some minutes, fingering all the gimmicks, wishing the car belonged to me.

Do me a favour . . . drop dead.

I got out of the car, then as I was about to close the garage swing down door, I saw the length of the car was just that much longer than the Plymouth and the door wouldn't close. I got back into the car, started the motor, then edged the car forward until the front bumper touched the end wall. Leaving the motor running, I got out of the car to check if the door would now close. It did, but only just. I slammed down the garage door, then as I walked back along the length of the car to turn off the motor, I became aware of the smell of fumes from the exhaust. Even while I had been checking the garage door and then shutting it, the build-up of fumes was surprising. I leaned into the car, turned off the motor, then opening the side door that led into the kitchen, I moved into the house.

Beth wasn't in the kitchen. I guessed she was somewhere in the big garden. I walked along the passage and into the living-room.

Marshall had found another bottle of whisky. He was sitting at the oval table by the window, papers spread before him and as I walked in, he poured a big shot of Scotch into a glass.

" Sit down, Keith." He waved to a chair by the table. " You know a million dollars sounds fine, but when you get all these goddamn taxes, a million shrinks."

" That's a fact, Frank." I sat down, " But it is still money. You should have at least six hundred thousand to call your own by the time the tax boys have taken you to the cleaners. If you invest a sum like that, you get income and capital appreciation."

" I don't need to be told." He sat back and stared glassily at me. " I'm onto a real hot tip : Charrington steel. The stock now stands at $15. I know Pittsburgh steel are taking Charrington over. Some six years ago, they tried, but came up against a S.E.C. rap, but I've got inside information that this time the merger is going through. Charrington steel shares will treble overnight."

I stared at him.

It had been Charrington steel that had landed me in jail. During the time I had spent in a cell I had often thought about that set-up and I realised that some of the members of the board had spread the news of the merger so cleverly, so expertly that suckers, like me, had been caught. Now, it seemed, they were at it again. They had let six years slide by: now according to this fat drunk, they were at it again: beating the drum, whispering about a merger, forcing up the stock price.

" Now, wait a minute, Frank," I said. " I know all about Charrington steel: that's one company you don't invest in. They're crooked. That merger will never jell."

He squinted at me.

" I know what I'm talking about. I've had a straight tip. What do you know about it?"

" Six years ago, they tried to merge with Pittsburgh. They spread the tale and the punters moved in. S.E.C. killed it and thousands of punters lost their money and I was one of them. Anyone crazy enough to speculate in that stock will get caught . . . no fooling, Frank."

" Is that right? Well, I know better." He finished his drink. " I know all about the suckers who were caught, but this time it is for real. I'm buying five hundred thousand dollars worth of stock as soon as I get probate. This is an inside tip. Jack Sonsan, the Vice-president of the company, is an old buddy of mine. I got the tip straight from him and he wouldn't twist *me!*"

I knew all about Jack Sonsan. Barton Sharman regarded him as one of the great con men of the century.

" Look, Frank," I said urgently. " I know what I'm talking about."

" Go help Beth in the garden," Marshall snapped, a sudden mean expression in his eyes. " Don't sit around here. I've work to do."

That was telling me I was, after all, the hired help and he didn't want any advice from me.

" Anything you say, Frank." I got up as he poured another drink, " But you're going to lose your money."

" That's what you say." He pointed a finger at me. " Listen, son, I know more about money than you'll ever learn. When I want advice from you, I'll shout for it . . . when I want advice."

The thought of him sinking five hundred thousand dollars into this mythical merger turned me sick. He had said the million would shrink after taxes had been paid. If he put five hundred thousand into Charrington steel he would be worth practically nothing.

" Frank, I . . ."

" Run along, son, I'm busy." He reached for a document. As I moved to the door, he went on, " You're okay with me, Keith. That car's a beaut. You make yourself useful around the house and look after the car. I'll look after the money."

" Just as you say, Frank."

He leaned back, his face flushed, the mean expression still in his eyes.

" Suppose we cut out the Frank thing, huh?" He reached for his glass and took a long drink. " Suppose we say Mr. Marshall, huh? No unfriendly feelings . . . just status symbol, huh?"

" Why sure, Mr. Marshall."

We looked at each other.

He laughed: an uneasy, embarrassed laugh.

" Go along with me, son. I'm feeling like a millionaire."

You fat, drunken sonofabitch, I thought, I'll go along with you only because I want to screw your wife.

" Sure, Mr. Marshall."

He nodded, then began to read the document.

I left him and walked out into the garden.

It was a big garden with shrubs, trees, flower beds and some of it jungle. Eventually, I found Beth picking raspberries at the far end of the garden. I came upon her as she was dropping fruit into a white bowl.

" I was told to come out here and help you in the garden . . . son," I said, pausing at her side.

She looked sharply at me.

" Has he got to calling you that?"

" That's it and I'm to call him Mr. Marshall because he is now a millionaire and I'm the hired help. Status symbol, he calls it."

She continued to pick raspberries. I sat on my heels, feeling the sun on my back and watched her.

" Beth . . . he has a wildcat scheme. He is going to put his money into a share investment that will lose him the bulk of the money."

She paused, her fingers red with the juice of the over-ripe fruit, and she looked searchingly at me.

" Although he is a drunk, Keith, he is smart. I've told you that already."

" Maybe, but he is sold on an investment in steel that can only bring disaster. He is going to buy shares as soon as he gets credit . . . at the end of next week."

She continued to stare at me.

" He's smart," she repeated.

" But I know this will be a disaster! I was once caught in the same trap! It looks fine, but it just won't and can't jell. He's going to lose every cent of the money that's coming to him . . . and you'll lose it too."

She began picking raspberries again. I watched her. Her face was as animated as a death mask.

After some minutes, I said, " Are you concentrating, Beth?"

" Yes." She turned to face me, holding the bowl of fruit against her tiny breasts. " You are really sure what he is planning will go wrong?"

" I am certain."

" And you can't persuade him to change his mind?"

" Not a chance."

She nodded, then began to pick more fruit. Again I watched her for some minutes, then I said, " What's going on in your mind, Beth?"

Without looking at me and continuing to pick the fruit, she said, " I was thinking it is a pity he isn't dead."

That cold dead finger ran up my spine. Here it is, I thought, and this time from her.

Do me a favour . . . drop dead.

Now she was saying it.

When he was dead, she would get his money and I would get her, but time was running out. When he got the money, he would lose it in this wildcat investment.

" There will be no money, Beth, unless he drops dead."

Her face wooden, she began on the second row of raspberry canes.

" Beth ! "

" Not now . . . tonight."

We looked at each other. Her black eyes were remote.

" Okay. Will you come to me ? "

She nodded.

I stood up and walked through the garden and back to the house. Through the open window his voice came clearly. He was talking on the telephone.

" . . . check the deeds," he was saying. " I can buy in a couple of weeks. I have this big stock deal cooking. Yeah . . . you get your end straightened out. I'll be ready in around fifteen days."

I don't think you will, Mr. Marshall, I thought as I moved quietly up the stairs. In fifteen days, you should be in a coffin.

*   *   *

I spent the rest of the afternoon, lying on the bed, my mind busy.

Even Marshall's heavy rumbling voice as he talked continuously on the telephone didn't distract my thinking.

As I smoked cigarette after cigarette, I told myself this was my second chance to move into the big money. My first chance had flopped and I had landed in jail, but this time it would be different. Instead of gambling with another man's money, I was now prepared to take a life. I had no compunction about getting rid of this fat drunken slob, yakking on the telephone downstairs. Already an idea how I could get rid of him in safety was beginning to jell. It would have to look like an accident, and then I would get Beth as well as the money.

The more I considered the idea the more I liked it, and finally, I convinced myself it was easy and safe and now convinced, my next move was to convince Beth. From what she had said : *I was thinking it's a pity he doesn't die,* I didn't think she would need much convincing.

The clock downstairs was chiming seven as I got off the bed. I went along to the bathroom, had a shave and then regarded myself in the mirror over the toilet basin. I looked as I always looked, but I knew behind the face looking back at me, I had become something I had never thought I was going to become : a killer.

I smelt frying onions. I went down the stairs and into the kitchen. She was standing over the stove, steaks on the grill, onions spluttering in the frypan.

" Smells good," I said, pausing in the doorway.

She nodded, her expression dead pan. I saw there were only two steaks under the grill.

Lowering my voice, I asked, " Where is he ?"

" In there . . . dead to the world."

" Should I get him to bed ?"

" Leave him where he is . . . later, perhaps." She turned the steaks.

Leaving her, I walked quietly into the living-room. He was sitting at the table, papers strewn before him, his open eyes fixed and sightless, his breathing heavy and slow.

" Mr. Marshall ?"

I went close and touched him. There was no reaction. I passed my hand before his open eyes : no blink : dead to the world was right. The bottle of Scotch, now empty, stood on the table.

Standing behind him, in case he suddenly came to the surface, I looked over his shoulder at the papers before him. There was a property deed: a house called 'Whiteoaks' in Carmel, along with a lot of scribbling, figures and names that meant nothing to me.

She came quietly into the room.

"Let's eat," she said.

I again touched him and again got no response, so I joined her in the kitchen. We sat, facing each other.

"We should get a doctor to look at him, Beth," I said as I began to cut into the steak. "It could be important."

She stared at me, then nodded.

"Let's give him half an hour, then if he hasn't come out of it, I'll call Dr. Saunders."

"Your local man? How bright is he?"

"He's been around for forty years: strictly a horse and buggy doctor."

We looked at each other and this time, I nodded. We finished the steaks and then ate raspberries and cream. We had coffee. Neither of us had anything to say. My mind was busy and I could see by that remote look in her black eyes, her mind was busy too. We enjoyed the meal as we listened to his heavy breathing coming from the living-room. I hoped the breathing might suddenly stop. I was sure she hoped the same, but we didn't trade confidences.

The meal over, I returned to the living-room and this time I took hold of his shoulder and shook him. He fell forward and I only caught him in time to prevent him sliding out of his chair onto the floor.

Beth had come to the door and was watching.

"Call the quack," I said.

She went out into the hall and I heard her dialling on the extension.

I got hold of Marshall and heaved him over my shoulder. He groaned, tried to come alive, then began to snore. Somehow, my heart thumping, I carried his bulk up the stairs and slung him on his bed. I loosened his collar, stripped off his jacket and took off his shoes.

She appeared in the doorway.

" He's on his way."

We stood over the fat body, listening to the stentorian breathing. We looked at each other. It would be so easy to shift the pillow and smother him, but that wouldn't be safe. I tossed a blanket over him and we went downstairs.

" He'll survive," I said as I moved into the living-room.

" Drunks are hard to kill."

I looked sharply at her, but her expression was again dead pan.

Fifteen minutes later while I was prowling around the living-room and Beth was clearing up in the kitchen, Dr. Saunders arrived in a 1965 Ford: a tall, stork like man with a bushy white moustache, wearing a battered panama hat and a crumpled grey suit.

I kept out of the way.

I heard Beth and him talking in the bedroom: just a murmur of voices, then after a while, they came down the stairs while I stayed out of sight in the kitchen. I heard his car start up and drive away.

" He said there was nothing the matter with him that can't be cured by a good sleep," she said as I came out of the kitchen.

" That's what we want to hear," I said. " So, fine . . . let him sleep it off."

It was dark by now, but the air was still and hot. There was a big moon that lit up the garden. I took her arm and we went out into the garden and walked away from the house. Screened by rose bushes and flowering shrubs, we sat on the hot, dry grass, shoulder to shoulder, facing away from the house.

If I was going to do this thing, I had to be sure of her and sure of the money.

" If something happened to him, Beth," I began, " would you want to marry me?"

That was giving it to her straight.

" Why talk about it?" she said. " Drunks last forever."

" So let's suppose he doesn't. Would you want to marry me?"

She nodded, then said, " Yes."

" Would you want to stay on here . . . live like a loner, do nothing but keep the house clean and work in the garden?"

" What else would you suggest I do?"

" With his money, Beth, I could become a Big shot. I could treble the money in a year or so. We could have a big house, staff, mix with important people. You would have a completely new kind of life. Would you want that?"

" Perhaps . . . I would have to think about it. Yes . . . I'm getting bored with this place. With you to help me . . . yes."

That was one hurdle jumped.

" Are you sure, Beth?"

She dropped her hand on mine.

" Can one ever be sure? But why talk about it?"

" In another two weeks he'll have invested in those steel shares and bang goes all the money. You said it was a pity he doesn't die. You said that, didn't you?"

She nodded.

" Didn't you?"

" Yes."

" Did you mean it?"

" Yes."

" Do you still mean it?"

" Yes."

" Well, he could die."

" But, how?"

" You know what this means, Beth?"

She leaned back on her elbows and stared up at the moon.

" I'm asking you, Keith . . . how?"

" Never mind right now about how. I want you to tell me that you realise what we are going to do." I paused, then said slowly and distinctly, " We are going to murder him."

That was as straight as I could give it to her. Now, it was up to her.

" But how?" she repeated.

" This doesn't scare you, Beth? That you and I will murder him?"

" Must you keep harping on that word?" There was an edge to her voice.

" I want you to realise what you and I are walking into. The pay-off is around six hundred thousand dollars, and you get me and I get you and we will share his money, but it will be murder."

She dropped flat on her back and put her hands over her eyes against the white light of the moon.

" Beth?"

" If we have to kill him, then we'll kill him."

I looked at her. Her hands covered her face. I reached out and pulled her hands away. In the light of the moon, her face looked as if it were carved out of marble.

" That's what we are going to do," I said.

She pulled free and again shielded her face with her hands.

" How will you do it, Keith?" Her voice was so low I scarcely could hear her.

" You too," I said. " I can't swing this on my own. Both of us, Beth. It'll be easy and safe so long as you accept the fact that we are going to murder him . . . do you?"

She moved her long legs in the grass.

" Yes."

I drew in a long, deep breath.

" Okay. I want to see his will."

" You can see it. I know where he keeps it."

" I want you and I want his money, Beth. Is that understood?"

" Yes."

" And you want me, Beth?"

She nodded.

" Have you seen his new car?"

She removed her hands and looked at me, surprised.

" No."

" We'll take a look at it. It's a beaut and it is going to kill him."

In the moonlight, side by side, we walked towards the garage.

six

I was in the kitchen, watching Beth frying eggs and bacon when we heard his heavy footfalls as he came down the stairs. We looked at each other, then I moved quickly into the living-room as he opened the door and came in.

There was a surly expression on his fat face and his eyes were bloodshot, but considering the state he had been in the previous night, he didn't look all that bad.

" Hi, Mr. Marshall," I said, keeping my voice low. I guessed he would have a hell of a hangover.

He grunted, then moved into the kitchen.

" Just coffee," he said.

Then he returned to the living-room.

" I've got a date in 'Frisco. I want to catch the early train."

That left less than forty minutes to get to the station : so good-bye breakfast.

Beth heard and turned off the stove. The eggs and bacon I had been looking forward to came to a spluttering halt. She served coffee. Scowling, Marshall stood with his back to the room and stared out of the window while he sipped the coffee.

" Get the car," he said without looking round.

Leaving my coffee half finished, I got the car from the garage. I had to wait some minutes before he appeared. Carrying a heavy briefcase, he slumped into the passenger's seat and I drove off.

After a while, he seemed to relax.

" This is a goddamn fine car!" he said. " I'll tell you something. A car like this is better than any woman. I'm sweating my guts out to drive her!"

" It won't be long now, Mr. Marshall."

He twisted around to stare at me.

" Skip the mister routine, Keith. I was in a mean mood yesterday. Call me Frank."

" Why sure, Frank," I said, thinking: You'll soon be dead, you drunken sonofabitch.

" Just remember one thing," he went on. " Don't shoot off your mouth to me about money. I know more about money than you'll ever learn."

Somehow I kept my face expressionless.

" Anything you say, Frank, but you did say I could be helpful."

" I know what I said, but I was drunk." He leaned forward and turned on the stereo radio.

End of the conversation.

There were a number of commuters getting out of their cars in the station parking lot as I drove up. They all paused to stare enviously at the Caddy and then they waved to Marshall. He ignored them.

Joe Pinner appeared from the station, carrying a heavy package. He dumped the package and came up fast as Marshall got out of the car.

" Hey, Frank! I've been wanting to have a word with you."

Ignoring him, Marshall said to me, " I'll be back on the six o'clock. Be here," then side-stepping Pinner as if he was the invisible man, he walked into the station.

Pinner stared after him, his expression shocked and hurt.

" Don't let it bother you, Joe," I said. " He has a hell of a hangover."

Tugging at his moustache, aware the other commuters were watching, Pinner moved up to me.

" Well, that was kind of rude."

Lowering my voice, I said, " Strictly between you and me, Joe, he was so drunk last night, Mrs. Marshall got scared and called in Dr. Saunders." I knew it would be news all over the town by midday, if not before.

His eyes popped wide open.

" Is that right?"

" But say nothing to nobody, Joe."

" Yeah. Well . . ."

I nodded to him, then drove from the station. In the driving mirror, I saw he was already talking to a couple of commuters and more of them were converging on him. The word would spread like a forest fire, and that's what I wanted.

Beth was making the beds when I got back. She came to the head of the stairs when she heard me enter the hall.

" Do you want breakfast, Keith?"

" Not now. I'll heat up some coffee."

" I'll be down in a minute."

I was drinking the coffee when she came into the kitchen. She was wearing shapeless slacks and an old, well-worn sweater, but there was still that thing about her that hooked me. Staring at her, I was sure if I got her dressed right, got her a new hair style, put her in the hands of people who knew how to make any woman look glamorous, she would be custom made for the wife of a millionaire : me !

" What are you staring at?" she asked uneasily.

I smiled at her.

" You . . . imagining you in three months' time. There'll be a big change."

She shrugged.

There was a pause, then I said, " Show me his will."

She went to the bureau, opened a drawer and took out a bundle of papers. She searched through them and finally handed me a single sheet of paper.

The will couldn't have been more simple. He left everything to her: the house, his business, his money. There were no bequests. She had it all. His sprawling signature was witnessed by Yule Olson and Maria Lukes, probably Olson's secretary.

I looked at Beth.

" He has no relations? No one who would contest this?"

" No."

The will was dated three years ago.

" It was my wedding present," she told me.

I re-read the will. It looked watertight. Marshall had begun to drink a year after he had married: that was common knowledge. If he had changed his will secretly since he had begun to drink, she could contest it was drunken irresponsibility and as there was no one to make a claim, she had to win. It looked fine to me. I handed the sheet of paper back to her.

" As soon as his aunt's will has been proved, Beth, we'll fix him."

She regarded me, her black eyes remote.

" It could take months."

" It won't take long to prove the will. Once the will has been proved, he inherits. There will be taxes and duties to take care of, but once the will is proved he becomes the heir and that means he can get any amount of credit while waiting for the estate to be settled. He is already buying the car on credit. Once he has been recognised as the legal heir to a million dollars, we can fix him because you, as his widow, will automatically inherit should he die."

She continued to stare at me.

" Are you sure?"

" I'm telling you."

She nodded, then put the will among the papers and the papers back in the bureau drawer.

" Once the will is proved, Beth, we kill him." I was determined she must realise just what I was planning to do.

Again the dead pan stare and the remote eyes as she nodded.

" You understand?" I said.

She turned away and moved to the door.

" Beth! You understand?"

She looked over her shoulder, nodded again, then leaving the room, she went up the stairs. After a second or so, I heard her bedroom door close.

Because Marshall meant nothing to me except money, I was being cold blooded about this, but surely, I thought, he must mean something to her. After all, she was his wife . . . she had slept with him.

But to her, it would seem we were planning nothing more important than drowning a cat. For all I knew, she might have had more feeling for the cat.

Again the cold dead finger moved up my spine.

Leaving the house, I wandered uneasily into the garden. I told myself that this was my second chance to achieve my ambition. I had to take this chance. I could never get a third one.

Away from the house, I sat on the grass, feeling the rays of the sun seep into me and I began to think what I would do once the money was mine. I was confident, once I got my hands on it, nothing and nobody could stop me from going to the top.

I lit a cigarette, then lying back on the hot grass, I let my mind drift into what could be an exciting future. I was still dreaming when Beth called that lunch was ready.

While we ate, I began to talk about our future together, but she cut me short. She seemed far away and her black eyes had that remote, cold expression.

" Later," she said curtly. " I don't want to talk about it now."

So we finished the meal in silence. As she began stacking the dishes, she said she was going to make jam, and if I had nothing to do, the lawn wanted cutting: her way of telling me she wanted to be alone.

The power mower was in the garage. I had left the Caddy out under the trees. I went to the garage by the kitchen door that led down a short passage to the garage. I paused to look at the lock on the garage door. The screws were rusty : a good solid kick would bust the lock.

The set-up was that you drove into the garage, pulled down the swing door and locked it. Then you unlocked the door leading to the kitchen and locked it from the other side. My first thought was to buy a bolt so the door into the kitchen was secure, but I quickly realised a new bolt would raise suspicions. The door itself was sound and solid. Then I walked into the garage and looked at the lock on the swing down door. This looked fragile.

I dragged the power mower out onto the lawn and after a struggle, got it going. As I tramped up and down the big lawn, my mind was busy. Finally, I decided two wooden wedges would be the answer.

I finished cutting the lawn by 16.00 and then went up to my room. I showered and put on a clean shirt. The smell of raspberries cooking filled the house. I could hear Beth's transistor playing classical music. Going down to the kitchen, I found her fixing caps on a dozen or so jars.

" You've made enough jam to stock a store," I said.

" I like doing it." She didn't look at me. She began cleaning the big copper pan in which she had made the jam.

Her remoteness began to worry me.

" Is something wrong, Beth ?"

She shook her head.

" No . . . it's just that I'm used to being on my own."

" But you are not on your own . . . you have me."

She went on scrubbing the pan.

" Are you telling me I'm in the way ?" I said sharply.

" It'll be different when I get away from this house."

" You bet it will be different."

I moved up to her and kissed the back of her neck. She shivered and jerked away from me.

" Do find something to do," she said, an edge to her voice. " I'm busy."

I struggled to keep my hands off her. After a long moment while I stared at her long, beautiful back, I went out, feeling thoroughly frustrated, got in the Caddy and drove down to Wicksteed. I was half an hour too early for the 18.00 'Frisco express so I bought a newspaper, sat in the car and tried to interest myself in the news, but I kept thinking of her.

As a woman in bed, she was the best ever, but I began to wonder about marrying her. I was sure she was a screwball, and she was also a loner, but if I didn't marry her, I wouldn't get the money. I began to realise I could have a problem on my hands.

I was so preoccupied with my thoughts I didn't hear the train arrive, but the noise made by the commuters as they got in their cars alerted me.

Marshall, carrying his brief-case, was coming down the slope towards me. I started the motor and drove up to him.

He looked sober and pleased with himself as he got in beside me.

" Did you have a good day, Frank?" I asked as I drove out of the parking lot.

" Yeah. And you . . . what did you do?"

" I cut the lawn."

He gave his bellowing laugh.

" That's Beth's favourite job. What did she do?"

" Made raspberry jam."

" That's her. Who the hell wants jam?" He shoved his hat to the back of his head. " Stop off at Olson's office. I want a word with him."

I parked outside Olson's office block and Marshall, carrying his brief-case, went in. I lit a cigarette and waited.

It was a good half hour before Marshall joined me. As he dropped into the passenger's seat, he gave a chortling laugh.

" That's fixed the old jerk," he said. " I've taken my business, including my aunt's will, out of his hands. My man in

'Frisco will handle everything from now on. He's a real live wire. Olson doesn't know what action means."

Alert, I said, " He's a horse and buggy lawyer."

" You're damn right. Harry Bernstein is the best."

I registered the name.

" Tomorrow, Keith, I want you to drive me to 'Frisco. I've got a lot cooking. We could be there three or four days and I'll want you to drive me around."

" Anything you say, Frank."

He patted my knee.

" We could have a little night fun, huh? Have you any liquor on board?"

I opened the glove compartment and handed him the bottle of Scotch. He was still sucking at the bottle when I drove up to the house.

He screwed on the bottle cap and handed the bottle to me.

" You know my trouble, Keith?" He grinned owlishly. " I drink too much."

I put the half empty bottle back into the glove compartment. I wasn't going to tell him I hoped he would drink himself to death.

" But you can take it, Frank."

That seemed to please him. He laughed.

" You're right. I can drink any guy under any table."

He heaved himself out of the car and went into the house. I put the Caddy away, then went up to my room.

I remained up there, lying on the bed, until Beth called up that dinner was ready.

*　　　*　　　*

The following morning, we left for 'Frisco. Marshall sat in the back of the car. He said he had reading to do. So we did the trip in silence. When we approached the City, he put his papers away and directed me to the Raven motel which was a couple of blocks from the Civic centre. He booked in while I stood around, then we walked to the two cabins and he told me to take it easy as he had telephone calls to make, so I sat in the cabin, watching a Soap opera on TV.

Around midday, he came into my cabin and dropped heavily into a chair. He had brought with him a bottle of whisky which he waved at me. I went to the refrigerator, got ice, found glasses and made him a heavy shot. I went light myself.

"Keith . . . you said you once worked with Barton Sharman," he said, relaxing after a long pull at his glass. "Can you steer me to someone high up who can talk credit?"

I slopped my drink. If he talked to anyone at Barton Sharman and if he mentioned my name, he would be told fast enough that I had served a jail sentence and Barton Sharman regarded me as all kinds of a leper.

"That was more than six years ago, Frank," I said. "Anyway, I'd choose Merrill Lynch rather than Barton Sharman."

"You would?" He finished his drink, blew out his cheeks, then shoved the glass at me for a re-fill. "I want credit, Keith. I thought you having worked with Barton Sharman, could swing something for me."

"Credit for what?"

"This Charrington steel deal. I want to start buying right now. Do you think Merrill Lynch would give me credit?"

"I don't know, Frank, but I'll tell you right away Barton Sharman never give credit. So you still want to go ahead with this steel deal?"

He accepted the re-fill, eyed me, drank, emptied his glass and got to his feet.

"Let's go. I've got a busy day ahead."

"Frank . . . this Charrington steel deal . . ."

He brushed by me and walked out into the sunshine and got in the Caddy.

All right, you stupid, drunken sonofabitch, I thought as I slid under the driving wheel, I'll fix you before you can lose your money.

We stopped off at Ghirardelli square for lunch. The waiters beamed on Marshall as he swaggered in and they had a corner table for him. We had Cioppino, a cross between a soup and a stew, made of all kinds of seafood. I neither liked nor disliked it, but Marshall had a second helping, washing it down with whisky.

" I've got to talk to Harry Bernstein," he said as he kept shovelling food into his mouth. " You stick around. I've got a lot to do. I'm selling out my real estate business."

After coffee, he got the check, paid and we went out to the Caddy. He directed me and I was lucky to find parking.

" Stick around. Maybe I'll be an hour."

I watched him, carrying his brief-case, walk into a big complex. I turned on the radio and waited, my mind busy.

Worked right, he just might get credit with Merrill Lynch and if he did, he would buy Charrington steel. The sooner he was dead, the better for Beth and myself.

While I sat in the Caddy, half listening to the radio, I wondered what Beth was doing.

If we have to kill him, then we'll kill him.

But time was now running out. If he bought those shares . . . !

Then I saw him with a short, fat man in a blue suit, a panama hat on the back of his head, a flowered tie and a cigar stuck in his mouth. They walked together down the sidewalk and approached the Caddy. I slid out and had the passenger's door open as they arrived.

" This is Keith Devery, Harry," Marshall said. " Keith, this is Harry Bernstein."

A cold, dry hand gripped mine.

We looked at each other.

" I've heard about you, Devery," he said. His voice was soft and husky.

114

A fat, flat face with eyes like glass beads, a small thin mouth, a sparrow hawk of a nose. A red light flashed up in my mind : this was a man to be handled with care.

" Let's go," Marshall said. " End of the street, second on the right, third on the left."

They got in the back and I set the car moving. Following his directions, we arrived outside a big complex.

" Stick around Keith," Marshall said and the two men got out and entered the complex.

I lit a cigarette, turned on the radio and thought about Harry Bernstein. Just under the hour they came out and got in the car.

" Take me back to the motel," Marshall said, " then take Harry back to his office."

" Sure, Frank," I said, the perfect chauffeur.

I decanted Marshall at the motel. He shook hands with Bernstein, then went to his cabin. Bernstein slid into the passenger's seat by my side and lit a cigar.

As I started the car, he said, " Frank was telling me about you, Devery. So you were with Barton Sharman ?"

" That's right . . . some five years ago." The red light began to flash.

" You have to be a smart cookie to work for that outfit."

" I guess that's right."

" Tell me something, Devery." He blew rich smelling smoke. " I've never met Mrs. Marshall . . . you have. What kind of woman is she ?"

If this fat Jew thought I was going to discuss Beth with him, he had another think coming.

" Ask Mr. Marshall," I said.

" Yeah, but you know Frank's a smart drunk and he doesn't talk. She interests me."

" I may not be smart, Mr. Bernstein and I'm no drunk," I said woodenly. " Your interest in Mrs. Marshall is no business of mine and that's the way I like to keep it."

" That makes you smart," Bernstein said and laughed.

I didn't say anything. We drove down the street leading to his office and I parked outside his office block. He seemed in no hurry to get out of the car. He twisted around in his seat and regarded me.

" I like Frank," he said, rolling his cigar around in his mouth. " He drinks a hell of a lot too much, but he has financial flair. Do me a favour, will you?"

Surprised, I stared at him.

" What favour?"

" He has taken to you. I get the idea he isn't happy with his wife. You're living with them. You can see the photo. I also have an idea she would be glad to be rid of him . . . I could be wrong, but watch him, Devery. If something that looks like trouble starts, let me know . . . huh?"

I felt a cold creepy feeling run up my spine.

" Trouble? What do you mean?"

He stared thoughtfully at me.

" If he could keep sober, he could turn his million into three million and more. He has a flair. Suppose you try to stop him from drinking? Suppose you keep his wife out of his hair? He told me he wants you to grow with him. If you want to grow, and you could grow with him, look after him. He needs looking after."

Giving me a curt nod, he got out of the car and walked across the sidewalk to his office block.

Did he suspect something? He had never seen Beth. So why had he said he had an idea she would be glad to be rid of Marshall? Something Marshall had said? Did Marshall suspect something?

With a growing feeling of uneasiness, I drove back to the motel.

" What did you think of Bernstein?" Marshall asked as I looked into his cabin. He was working at a table, papers spread out, the inevitable bottle of whisky at hand.

" Smart," I said, lingering in the doorway.

" You're right . . . dead smart. He's going to swing this

credit deal for me with Merrill Lynch." He grinned. " I start buying tomorrow."

Although my heart skipped a beat, I kept my face expressionless.

" What does Mr. Bernstein think of this deal, Frank?"

He laughed.

" Harry knows as much about making money as you do. I don't need his advice."

" Well, it's your money. Don't say I didn't warn you, Frank."

" Take time off." He waved me away. " See you around eight o'clock." He winked. " We might have some night fun. Let's look at the whores, huh?"

" Fine," I said and left him.

Shutting myself in my cabin, I telephoned Merrill Lynch's branch office and asked to speak to a broker.

" Sanderstead," a voice said. " Can I help you?"

" My name is Tom Jackson," I said. " I'm thinking of investing thirty thousand dollars. I had a tip to buy Charrington steel for a big rise. There's talk of a merger with Pittsburgh. What do you think?"

A pause, then he said, " We have no information about a merger, Mr. Jackson, and we regard Charrington steel as highly speculative. In fact, we wouldn't recommend this stock. Can I interest you ..."

I had heard all I wanted to hear. If Merrill Lynch considered Charrington steel as highly speculative and didn't know of any merger, my own opinion was confirmed. I replaced the receiver.

I sat still, asking myself how I was going to stop this drunken fool from throwing away the money that was to come to Beth and to me.

The idea of spending a night with him and whores sickened me. I decided I would beg off, tell him I had a stomach upset. If he didn't like it, he could go to hell.

I lay on the bed, my mind seething. I began to wonder if I

could kill him right now before he bought the stock, but no
safe ideas came to me. Finally, around 18.00, I went into his
cabin ready to tell him I was sick, but as I entered the cabin,
I saw there was no need.

He lay on the bed, the whisky bottle empty by his side and
he was dead to the world: so dead looking I wondered, with
a surge of hope, if he had died.

Going over to him, I shook him. He muttered something,
groaned, then became unconscious again. I dragged open his
collar, then stood back, staring at him. He looked bad. I had
him at my mercy, but this wasn't the time. Crossing to the
telephone, I asked the booking clerk to get a doctor.

" Mr. Marshall isn't well."

The word had reached 'Frisco that Marshall was now worth
a million dollars so I got service. After a while a doctor arrived:
lean, alert, youngish.

" There's nothing I can do for him," he said after a careful
examination. " Get him undressed. He will sleep it off. Would
you like me to send a nurse?"

" I can manage," I said. " I look after him."

He produced some pills.

" Give him these tomorrow." A pause, then he went on, " If
he continues to drink like this, he will kill himself."

" I'll tell him," I said woodenly.

When he had gone, I decided it would be smart to call
Harry Bernstein. When I got him on the line, I told him what
had happened and what the doctor had said.

" Do you want me to come over, Devery?" he asked. He
sounded worried.

" No, there's no need. He usually pulls out of it," I said.
" He could be as bright as a goddamn cricket by tomorrow
morning. I'll watch him."

" I hope he is. We have two important business meetings to
handle tomorrow. Telephone my home around eight tomorrow
morning will you?" and he gave me a number.

I said I would and hung up. I took another look at Marshall.

He was still dead to the world. I looked around the cabin, saw his big brief-case and crossed over to it, but it had a substantial lock. Nothing short of busting the lock would open it without a key and I didn't feel like going through his pockets.

I spent the rest of the evening watching TV with the sound turned down and with half an eye on the unconscious man. Around nine o'clock his breathing settled to a heavy snore and I reckoned he would be all right if I left him.

I went along to the restaurant, had a prawn salad, then after looking at him and finding him still sleeping, I went to bed.

I had been asleep for three or four hours when the sound of my door opening brought me awake. I flicked on the light.

Marshall was standing in the doorway. He looked like hell, his hair mussed, his face enflamed, his eyes watering.

" Get me a drink," he snarled. " Don't lie there, staring. I want a shot."

I remembered Bernstein's words. *Suppose you try to stop him drinking. If you want to grow with him, and you could grow with him, look after him.*

But I knew I could grow much, much faster without him.

" Sure," I said. " I've got a bottle in the car. I'll get it."

" Get it and get it fast," he growled, then staggered away back to his cabin.

I put on my shoes and in pyjamas, went to the car park and got the Scotch from the glove compartment. It was a hot, still night, and the only light showing came from Marshall's cabin.

He was standing in the doorway as I reached him. He grabbed the bottle, then slammed the door in my face.

Go ahead, you sonofabitch, I thought, drink yourself to death.

* * *

At 07.45 the following morning, I went to his cabin, knocked and walked in.

I was half expecting to find him up and dressed, but he was still in bed and he looked bad. The bottle of whisky, half empty, stood on the bedside table.

"Are you okay, Frank?" I asked, pausing in the doorway.

"I feel like hell." There was a whine in his voice. "I don't know what's the matter with me. I tried to get up but I can't stand. You'd better call a quack."

"Right. Just take it easy."

I went back to my cabin and called Bernstein at his home number. When I had explained the situation, not mentioning that I had given Marshall whisky at three o'clock this morning, Bernstein cursed softly, said he would come and for me to get the doctor.

He and the doctor arrived at the same time. They seemed to know each other. They went into Marshall's cabin. I decided to keep out of it so I stood around in the hot sunshine and waited.

After half an hour, they came out and the doctor shook hands with Bernstein, nodded to me, got in his car and drove away. Bernstein joined me.

"Frank wants to go home," he said. "Dr. Kersley thinks it's the best thing. Now listen, Devery, if there is any liquor in the house, get rid of it. Kersley says it is essential Frank doesn't have a drink for at least two days. I'm leaving it up to you. If he has another drinking jag, he'll be dangerously ill. Understand?"

"Is he fit to travel?" I asked, thinking at least Marshall wouldn't buy Charrington steel this day, and a day gained was a day won.

"Kersley has given him some pills. Don't drive fast. He'll be all right. When you get him home, call me at the office. Get him to bed. Let him have warm milk, no solids and no, repeat no, liquor." He looked at his strap watch. "Goddamn it! I'm already late. Look after him, Devery," and he hurried off to his car and drove away.

I went to my cabin, packed my bag, then went to the reception clerk and paid the check. I found Marshall sitting on the edge of the bed, his head in his hands. The bottle of whisky had vanished. I guessed he had been crafty enough to have put it out of sight so the doctor couldn't take it from him. I got him dressed with difficulty. He seemed dopey, probably the pills were working. He didn't say anything until I had finished packing his bag, then he said, " I'll be okay once I get home."

" Sure, Frank. Let's go."

He reached under the bed and produced the half bottle of Scotch.

" Put it in the glove compartment, Keith."

I had to help him walk to the car. He dropped into the passenger's seat and watched me while I put the whisky in the glove compartment.

" This is a hell of a time to get ill," he muttered as I started the motor. " I've so much to do."

" Take it easy." I drove out onto the highway. He fell asleep after I had driven a couple of miles and he was sleeping when I pulled up outside the big, lonely house.

A police car stood in the driveway. The sight of it gave me a shock. I got out of the Caddy and walked up the steps and pushed open the front door.

Standing in the hall was Deputy sheriff Ross. Standing in the living-room doorway was Beth.

I stared first at Beth, then at Ross. He was holding his Stetson by his side. There was a pause, then he moved forward, slapped the hat on his head, walked around me and down the steps towards the police car. I turned and watched him. He paused by the Caddy and looked at Marshall who was snoring, then he got into the police car, backed down the drive, then went shooting off down the dirt road.

" What's he doing here?" I asked Beth, my voice husky.

She grimaced, then shrugged.

"Checking on the Plymouth. He wanted to know if Frank had had it repaired. What are you doing back here? Frank said he would be away for four days."

The fact that Ross had been here somehow scared me.

"Didn't Ross know the Plymouth was sold?"

"Obviously not. Why else should he have come? Is Frank with you?"

"He's ill. He's sleeping in the car."

"Ill?" She regarded me with her black remote eyes. "What's the matter?"

"He drank too much last night. I'll get him in."

"Is he bad?"

We stared at each other.

"Not bad enough."

Again she grimaced, then went into the living-room and shut the door.

I had a struggle getting Marshall out of the car and up the stairs to his room. He flopped on the bed. I got his clothes off and got him into his pyjamas. He rolled under the sheet and as I stood over him, he stared up at me.

"Get me a drink, Keith."

"No drink, Frank. The doctor said . . ."

"Get me a drink!" A mean expression came over his face.

"Not now, maybe later, Frank."

"Hear me?" He half sat up. "I don't give a goddamn what any quack says. I want a drink!"

"Okay."

Leaving him, I went down the stairs and into the living-room. Beth was standing by the window. The clock in the hall struck six.

"How is he?" she asked without turning.

"He wants a drink." I went to the liquor cabinet and took out a bottle of whisky, half full, a glass and charge water. I went into the kitchen and added a little tap water to the bottle, then I went upstairs and put the bottle, charge water and glass on the bedside table. As he grabbed the bottle, I went out and down to the living-room. Beth still remained, her back turned, looking out of the window. I called Bernstein's office number.

" I got him home all right, Mr. Bernstein," I said. " He's resting right now."

" Fine. Keep him away from liquor, Devery. Call me tomorrow if there's any change. Have you a doctor handy?"

" No problem, Mr. Bernstein. I think he'll be okay tomorrow."

" Look after him," and Bernstein hung up.

Beth had come away from the window and was watching me, her dark eyes remote.

" We do it tonight, Beth," I said. " If he hadn't drunk so much last night he would have bought Charrington steel this morning. We can't afford to let him live any longer."

I waited for some reaction, but her expression remained dead pan.

" How will you do it?" Her voice was low.

" There's something I have to fix first before we talk," I said, and going through the kitchen I went into the garage. I found a thick strip of wood and after hunting through the tool box I found a wood axe. I made two wedges. I tried one of them under the door leading into the garage. The wedge was too thick. After chipping off more wood, it fitted. I did the same with the second wedge so it fitted under the swing up door. Leaving the garage, I went through the kitchen, through the hall and out into the garden. Going to the closed swing up door, I pushed in the wedge and kicked it home. Then I returned to the garage via the kitchen and shoved against the swing up door. It held firm against the wedge. I drew back and slammed my shoulder against the door. The wedge still held it firm. Satisfied, I went into the kitchen.

" Beth!"

She came quickly.

" I'm going into the garage and I'm shutting the door," I

said. " I want you to put this wedge under the door when it is closed and kick it home."

She stared briefly at me, then took the wedge. I went into the garage and shut the door. She did exactly what I had told her to do. When I heard her kick the wedge home, I turned the door handle and slammed my shoulder against the door. It held.

" Okay. Get the wedge out," I said.

She had trouble getting it out, but she got it out. I opened the door and joined her in the kitchen. I took the wedge from her and dropped it in my pocket.

" Let's go in the garden."

By now it was 19.20 and it was getting dusk. The air was still and hot with a hint of an approaching storm. We went together away from the house and we sat on the grass bank.

" What are you planning?" she asked, her voice tense.

" This may not work," I said. " If it works, it is safe. If it doesn't work, we must think of something else, but if it doesn't work we are still clear of trouble."

" Don't talk in riddles!" There was an edge to her voice. " Tell me!"

" Last night, he had me up at three o'clock demanding whisky. He told me to get the bottle from the glove compartment of the car. I'm gambling on the same thing happening tonight. If it does, then we've fixed him. If it doesn't, then as I said, we must try something else, but I'm pretty certain he'll need a drink sometime tonight when we are both supposed to be in bed. The idea is, sometime before we go to bed, I'm starting the car engine and I'm putting on the car heater. If he goes down to the garage to get the bottle, I'll be waiting and I'll wedge the door so he can't get out. There will be enough build up of carbon monoxide in the garage to kill him. We'll find him missing in the morning, hunt, find him in the garage. The picture will be obvious. He came down in his pyjamas, got in the car, found the bottle, felt chilly, turned on the engine and the heater and decided to stay until he had finished the bottle. Before he could do so the fumes fixed him. That's the plan, Beth. What do you think?"

She sat motionless. I didn't hurry her. After several minutes, she said, " Yes, but will he come down?"

" That's the gamble, but if he doesn't we are still in the clear. We will have to think of some other way, but this is the safest."

" Then let's try."

Again as if we were planning to drown a cat. No emotion, no nothing. Once more the cold dead finger went up my spine.

" The Sheriff will be up here, Beth, and Ross who is a troublemaker although it was lucky he was out here when we came back. He saw how drunk Frank was. Now listen, we must both say the same thing. We tell the Sheriff we heard nothing during the night. I went to bed soon after nine-thirty. I was tired after sitting up with him the previous night. You read until ten-thirty and then you went up. You looked in to see how he was. He was asleep and snoring. I intended to look in during the night, but I was so bushed I didn't wake until seven. When I found he wasn't in his bed, I woke you and we looked around and found him in the garage. We try to revive him. We call Dr. Saunders and the Sheriff, but Saunders first. I want him on the scene before the Sheriff arrives, then I call Bernstein."

She nodded, then said, " But he hasn't got probate yet."

" We can't wait. It'll be all right. You have his will. You inherit everything from him. Bernstein is tricky. He could be the danger man unless you handle him right. Your line is to play helpless. You need his advice. He'll like that. Show him the will and ask him if he will represent you. You're going to be a millionairess. You'll be important people to him and once he knows he is going to act for you, he's not going to be tricky. Get all that?"

" Yes."

" Okay, let's go over the details."

We spent the next hour working on the plan. I threw the

kind of questions the Sheriff might throw at her and she came
back word perfect. I could see I didn't have to worry about
her performance. She was as cold and as calm as the original
ice woman. Finally, I was satisfied and I found I was hungry.

" Let's eat," I said. " While you cook up something, I'll take
a look at him."

I quietly opened his bedroom door. The bedside lamp was
on and he was awake. The whisky bottle was empty.

" How do you feel, Frank?"

" I'm okay." His voice was a surly growl.

" Feel like something to eat?"

" No." He waved to the empty bottle. " Get rid of this and
bring me a fresh one."

" Sorry, Frank, no more drinking tonight. I've had strict
instructions. Mr. Bernstein is holding me responsible. The
doctor says you'll be dangerously ill if you have even one more
drink for two days."

His eyes turned mean.

" You're employed by me, not Bernstein!"

" I'm still sorry, Frank."

He regarded me, then a crafty expression came into his
eyes.

" I'll settle for a double and no bottle. How's about it?"

I pretended to hesitate, then I nodded.

" Well, okay, but that's the last you get."

" Stop gabbing. Go get it!"

I went downstairs, took out a full bottle of whisky, made a
double, then as Beth came to the door I handed her the bottle.

" Any more in the house?"

" That's the last one."

" Hide it and hide it good . . . in the garden."

I took the drink up to his room, added a shot of charge
water and gave it to him. He gulped it down and relaxed.

" I'll sleep now," he said. " Turn the light off."

I took the glass, turned off the light and went to the door.

" You'll be fine tomorrow, Frank."

He grunted and I closed the door.

I stood for a moment at the head of the stairs. With any luck he would be dead by tomorrow. I felt a tingle of excitement run up my spine. In a month or two, Beth and I would be worth a million!

I drew in a long deep breath, then went down to the kitchen.

seven

A LITTLE AFTER 21.00, I went into the garage. I again tested the swing up garage door. Held by the outside wedge, it was rock firm. Then I got into the Caddy and started the motor, also switching on the heater at quarter power. Getting out of the car, I shut and locked all the car doors. Marshall was to have no chance to turn off the engine.

There was a small pilot light above the door leading into the passage which automatically lit up when you opened the door leading into the passage or when you swung up the garage door. Moving into the passage, I shut the door, then went back to the living-room.

Beth was sitting as I had left her, motionless, her hands in her lap. She looked at me, her eyes remote.

" It's all set," I said. I looked at my watch. " I'm going up now. You stay here for an hour, then come up. Take a bath. If he is awake I want him to know you're going to bed. Stay in your room. From now on, I'll handle it."

She nodded.

" This is it, Beth. Do you still want to go ahead? With any luck you and I will be worth a million by tomorrow."

" Yes."

She was the ice woman again. A screwball, I thought, watching her, but without her, I couldn't get the money and that was all I was now thinking about.

" If he walks into the trap, Beth," I said at the door, " I'll tell you. Don't go to sleep. It could be a long wait."

Again she nodded.

Leaving her, I went up the stairs. Soundlessly, I eased open Marshall's door an inch or so. I could hear his heavy breathing and now and then a strangled snore. I went into my bedroom, turned down the bed, then changed my shoes for a pair of sneakers. Turning off the overhead light, I turned on the bedside lamp and sat in an armchair. Faintly, I could hear Marshall snoring. I wondered if he would sleep right through the night. If he did my plan was sunk.

I spent the next hour thinking about Beth and thinking about the money. I realised if Marshall were found dead to-morrow, I would have to leave the house. I couldn't remain here with Beth alone. There must be no head waggings or gossip about us in Wicksteed. I would go back to Mrs. Hansen, then when Beth knew she had control of the money, I would go to 'Frisco and wait for her to join me. The thought of being separated from her for at least a month bothered me, but I knew we had to play it safe.

Around 22.30, I heard her come up the stairs. Moving silently, I half opened my door and watched her go into her bedroom. I waited, hearing her moving around. She closed the closet door with a loud click, then she came out in a dressing gown and went into the bathroom, leaving the door ajar. She began to run the bath. If Marshall was awake he must hear these preparations for going to bed.

I turned off the bedside light, then switching on a small pocket flashlight, I reversed the key in the lock, stepped into the corridor and locked the door, removing the key.

The bath water had stopped running. The house was silent. I couldn't hear Marshall snoring. Had he woken? I went downstairs and into the living-room. I didn't turn on the lights, but using my flashlight, I went over to the window recess. I had already picked this as my hiding place. The recess was covered by heavy ceiling-to-floor curtains. There was room enough behind the curtains to take a chair. Pulling back the curtains, I carried a small armchair into the recess, then closed the curtains and sat down.

I was aware my hands were clammy and there were sweat beads on my face. All I now could hear was the rustle of leaves as the wind increased. I looked out of the window. The big moon was half hidden by drifting black clouds. The window was sprinkled with rain. I hoped there wouldn't be a storm. I wanted to hear every sound that went on in the house.

Parting the curtains, I sat forward and listened. I could hear Beth's bath water running away. Then I heard her bedroom door close. Then there was silence.

The wind began to whine around the house and the rain increased. Leaving the recess, I went into the hall. I had to hear if he got out of bed. I sat on the bottom stair and tried to relax.

I sat there for three tense, nerve wracking hours, continually looking at my strap watch. Apart from the sound of the wind and the rain, I heard nothing.

From time to time, I stood up and stretched, but I didn't move around as the wooden floor of the hall was old and creaked.

At 02.00, I began to worry. Maybe that last double whisky had fixed him and he would sleep until daylight. I wondered if Beth was awake. She was cold and indifferent enough to be sleeping. I listened to hear any snoring from Marshall, but could hear nothing, but the rain beating down. I longed to smoke, but resisted the temptation.

The clock in the living-room struck the half hour and I cursed to myself. The gamble wasn't going to work! Getting to my feet, and flicking on my flashlight, I returned to the window recess and sank into the armchair. I drew the curtains. The tension of waiting, the previous night's loss of sleep were taking their toll. I felt suddenly exhausted and desperately tired. My eyelids kept drooping. He hadn't fallen for the bait! I shouldn't have given him that whisky! Now, I would have to think of another scheme to get rid of him. My eyes closed. I was now too tired to care. I nodded off.

I woke with a start as the clock struck three.

The light was on in the living-room! Immediately alert, my heart pounding, I parted the curtains so I could see.

Marshall, in his pyjamas, was standing in the doorway, his hair mussed, his face inflamed, his eyes furtively searching the room. He moved unsteadily to the liquor cabinet, paused to listen, then opened the double doors. He peered in, then uttered a four-letter word. For a long moment he stared into the empty cabinet, then shut the doors. Again he looked around the room, then staggered out and towards the kitchen.

With my heart pounding, I went silently to the door. I watched him turn on the kitchen light. I could see his broad back as he went to the refrigerator, opened the door, peered in and again muttered the four-letter word. He shut the refrigerator door and stood motionless for several seconds, then he moved out of sight.

He was remembering the bottle of whisky in the Caddy's glove compartment. He had taken the bait!

Moving silently, I paused at the kitchen door, my hand in my pocket, my fingers around the wooden wedge. He had gone down the passage that led to the garage!

I moved into the kitchen. Sweat was bothering me, and with the back of my hand, I wiped it from dripping into my eyes. My heart was now pounding so violently I had trouble with my breathing. I could hear him stumbling down the passage to the garage door. I moved forward. I could see him as he opened the door leading into the garage. The pilot light came on and he started forward, then stopped.

" What the hell!" I heard him mutter. " The motor's running!"

He stood staring into the garage, his back to me. I realised he was sober enough to smell the build up of fumes. Even from where I stood, I could smell them.

If he turned around, I was sunk. In a blind panic, I rushed

forward, my hands outstretched. They slammed against his back, pitching him into the garage. Sweat blinding me, my breath rasping through my clenched teeth, I slammed the door shut, bent and shoved the wedge home.

I had scarcely time to kick the wedge into place when he thudded against the door.

"Get me out of here!" he bawled. "Beth! Hear me! Get me out of here."

Panting, I leaned hard against the door. Again he thudded his body against the door which creaked alarmingly, but held.

"Keith!" His voice sounded fainter.

I was cold and shaking. It couldn't last more than another minute or so, I told myself. Drop dead . . . drop dead!

Again he thumped on the door, but they were feeble little thumps now, then there was a slithering sound, as clawing at the door, he sank down.

I moved away from the door, took out my handkerchief and blotted my face. My legs were trembling. I became aware that Beth was standing at the end of the passage, watching.

"Go away!" I said huskily, hating her to see the state I was in. "Go away!"

She pulled her dressing gown around her, nodded and moved out of sight. I stood listening. All I could now hear was the steady beat of the car engine. I gave the wedge another kick, then moved back into the kitchen.

Beth was there, a glass of neat whisky in her hand. She thrust it at me. I drank, the glass rattling against my teeth.

We looked at each other.

"It's done," I said, only when the whisky began to bite. "Go to bed."

"Is he dead?" The flat, cold indifferent voice could have been querying if the cat I had drowned was dead.

"He will be. Not yet . . . he is unconscious, but in a few more minutes." I wanted another drink. Seeing the whisky bottle on the sink, I picked it up, but my hand was shaking so badly, I slopped whisky onto the draining board and not in the glass.

Beth took the bottle from me and poured the drink. Her hand was rock steady.

" Careful of that," she said. " I'll go back to bed now. We call Dr. Saunders at eight o'clock?"

I stared at her. Her utter indifference horrified and angered me.

" He's dying in there," I said, my voice cracking and out of control. " Doesn't it mean anything to you?"

Her remote eyes examined my sweating face.

" It was your idea," she said. " It wasn't mine. Go easy with the whisky," and turning, she went silently out of the kitchen as a sudden crash of thunder shook the house.

*　　*　　*

The clock downstairs struck seven.

For the past hours, I had been lying on my bed, my mind in a turmoil.

I had committed murder!

Planning a murder was one thing. While I had planned it, my mind was obsessed with Beth and money. Now I had done it, fear of the consequences swamped me. I told myself that Marshall would have died from drink anyway, but that didn't help. I thought of Beth. While we were making love, she was the most important thing in my life, but when I thought of her standing in the kitchen, cold, ruthless and utterly indifferent knowing Marshall was suffocating to death, my lust for her faltered.

I had brought the bottle of whisky up with me and I now reached for it, but as my hand hovered over it, I restrained myself. I was not going to become a lush like Marshall because of her.

I got off the bed, stripped off my shirt and went into the bathroom. I shaved and sloshed water over myself. Then putting on a clean shirt and my shoes, I opened the bedroom door. As I did so, Beth's door opened.

She had on the shapeless sweater and slacks and her hair was anyhow. Her face was pale, and there were dark rings under her eyes, but her expression was controlled and dead pan.

We looked at each other.

"I'll go down and open the garage door," I said. "The concentration of gas in there will be dangerous. We'll have to give it time to clear."

She nodded.

I went down, left the house and walked around to the garage. I pulled out the wedge and dropped it into my pocket. Then with my heart thumping, I swung up the garage door and stepped back. Peering into the garage, all I could see was the Caddy. He must be lying out of sight at the back of the car.

I returned to the house, went through the kitchen to the garage door and removed the second wedge. I went into the boiler room and dropped the two wedges into the oil furnace. As I started up the stairs, I saw her in the living-room, staring out of the window. She had removed the armchair from the recess and had put it back where it usually stood.

I took the bottle of whisky from my bedside table, emptied the contents down my toilet basin, then took the empty bottle into the kitchen and dropped it in the trash bin.

"Okay," I said. "Come on. It'll be safe enough now."

"You can do it," she said without turning.

"I can't handle him alone."

She didn't turn. Going to her, I gripped her arm.

"We're in this together!" I shouted at her. "Come on!"

She hunched her shoulders, then without looking at me, went into the kitchen. Moving ahead of her, I went down the passage and opened the garage door.

He was lying face down, his head close to the exhaust pipe. He looked as if someone had deliberately put him there.

Was he dead?

With a shaking hand, I took the car keys from my pocket, unlocked and opened the car door. The heat in the car hit me like a blow in the face. I slid in and turned off the motor, then reaching across, I opened the glove compartment and took out the half bottle of whisky, holding it by its neck. I had thought about this. Both Marshall and I had handled the bottle. I wasn't worried about my prints, but I wanted them to find his on the bottle.

Unscrewing the cap, I laid the bottle on the floor of the car. The whisky ran out making a stain on the lamb's wool carpet.

While I was doing this, Beth stood motionless in the doorway, her arms crossed while she stared fixedly at Marshall's body.

I got out of the car. Bracing myself, I went to him, knelt and dragged him over on his back. One look at him told me he was dead. His eyes were wide open and fixed. There were tiny flecks of foam around his mouth.

" We've got to get him into the car." My voice was a croak.

" Is he dead?"

" Look at him! Of course he's dead!"

I saw her shudder, then she came to me. Between us, we dragged him to the car door. While she held him, I went around and opened the passenger's door. Kneeling on the bench seat, I hauled him in while she pushed.

" Okay. Now call Saunders," I said. " Tell him we found him in here and you're sure he is dead. Tell him the motor was running and ask him what we should do."

She went away.

I let his body fall forward across the driving wheel. The car stank of whisky. Shutting the passenger's door, but leaving the driving door open, I walked into the fresh air. Lowering the garage door, I examined it to see if the wedge had left a mark. It hadn't. I went back into the garage and examined the door leading to the kitchen. There was a slight mark, but so slight as to be almost invisible. I was sure no one would notice it.

I then checked the whole set-up, knowing this was the last chance I would have before the Sheriff arrived.

It looked good with Marshall slumped over the driving wheel, the empty whisky bottle at his feet, the heater control on. It seemed to me the picture told its own story.

I went into the living-room. Beth was standing by the window, her back to me.

" What did he say?"

" To leave him how we found him. He's coming, and he is calling the Sheriff."

I went to her and swung her around.

" Now listen to me! Neither the Sheriff nor Bernstein have ever seen you. For God's sake, take that dead pan expression off your face! You have just lost your husband! Okay, you were sick of his drinking, but that doesn't mean you don't give a damn that he is dead! Try to show some emotion!"

She jerked free.

" And you get hold of yourself," she said in a low, hissing voice. " You looked frightened."

I was frightened! With an effort I pulled myself together.

" I'll call Bernstein." I went to the telephone and dialled his home number. When he came on the line, I told him that Marshall was dead and how it had happened.

Apart from a grunt or two, he listened and didn't ask questions.

" The doctor and the Sheriff are on the way," I said. " Could you get over here, Mr. Bernstein?"

" You're sure he is dead?"

" I'm sure."

" I'm coming," and he hung up.

Beth had gone into the kitchen. She came out with two cups of coffee.

" Be very careful how you handle Bernstein," I said. " He's coming. Remember he's the danger man."

" Don't keep on! I'll handle him!" Her voice was sharp.

We sipped the coffee.

"I won't be able to stay on here, Beth," I said. "I'll have to go back to Wicksteed. We can keep in touch by telephone. I'll call you every evening at half past eight from a call box. If there is an emergency, call Mrs. Hansen and say there's something wrong with the Caddy and you want me to come up."

She nodded.

"As soon as you know you're going to get the money, Beth, I'll move to 'Frisco. You stay on for a week or so, then put the house up for sale and then join me. Right?"

Again she nodded.

"I hate being away from you for so long, but there's no other safe way. No one must suspect what we mean to each other."

"Yes."

The flat, remote voice made me want to shake her.

At this moment Dr. Saunders arrived.

"I'll handle him," I said. "Don't forget you're shocked. Go upstairs and lie down. Keep out of the way until the Sheriff comes. You'll have to see him."

Her expression still dead pan, she went out of the room and up the stairs as I went to the front door.

Dr. Saunders regarded me. I explained who I was, said Mrs. Marshall was upset and wanted to be alone, then I took him to the garage and left him there.

I stood around, aware my hands were sweaty and my heart was beating unevenly. After ten minutes or so, he came out of the garage.

"We'll leave him as he is until the Sheriff arrives," he said.

Seeing an approaching cloud of dust on the dirt road I said, "He's coming now."

We waited. The Sheriff, with Ross at his side, pulled up outside the house.

I stood back while McQueen talked to Saunders, then he and Saunders, with Ross tagging behind, went into the garage.

I went into the living-room and sat down. I was pretty sure

I could handle McQueen, but I was uneasy of Ross. He was one of those smart bastards who would look for trouble.

I smoked four cigarettes before I saw, through the window, Dr. Saunders drive off. I smoked another three before I saw McQueen and Ross coming to the house. Ross carried the whisky bottle in a plastic sack.

I got to my feet and moved to the living-room door as they came into the hall.

" Where's Mrs. Marshall?" McQueen asked as I moved back and they came into the living-room.

" She's upstairs," I said. " This has been a shock. I'll get her if you want to talk to her."

" I'll talk to you first." McQueen pulled at his droopy moustache and selecting a chair, sat down. Ross put the bottle on the table, then sat down and took out a notebook. " Sit down, son," McQueen went on. " Suppose you tell us about it?"

I told him the story: how Marshall had employed me to drive his car, how we had gone to 'Frisco, of his continuous drinking, of his meeting with Bernstein, how Bernstein had asked me to keep liquor away from him, how he had got so drunk in 'Frisco I had to call a doctor, how Bernstein and the doctor decided he should go home, how I had driven him back, how he had demanded whisky and how I had told him Bernstein had made me responsible for keeping liquor out of his way. How, when I had got him to bed, I had thrown away the only full bottle of whisky in the house, but that I had forgotten there was a half bottle in the car's glove compartment. I went on to explain I had been up the previous night looking after him and I was bushed. I had gone to bed and slept through until the morning.

" Mrs. Marshall went to bed later. She looked in on Frank. He was sleeping. She went to bed," I said, looking straight at McQueen. " I guess during the night he woke up and remembered the whisky in the car, came down, found it chilly in the garage, turned on the engine and the heater . . . when I found

138

him the heater was on and the car suffocatingly hot . . . then he started drinking. I guess the fumes fixed him."

McQueen nodded.

I went on to tell him that we were both up around seven. I went to see how Marshall was, found the bed empty. We had searched the house and finally had found him in the garage. I had opened the garage doors, turned off the motor, made sure he was dead while Mrs. Marshall had called Dr. Saunders. I paused, then lifted my hands. " That's it, Sheriff."

McQueen digested this, stroking his moustache, then he looked at Ross.

" The facts add up, Abel," he said. " Suppose we now talk to Mrs. Marshall, huh?"

Ross stared steadily at him as he said, " Looks to me like an open and shut case, Chief." He closed his notebook. " As you say, the facts add up. If you want to disturb Mrs. Marshall at this time, that's your privilege."

I could scarcely believe my ears. I was expecting Ross to start all kinds of trouble, but instead, here he was, slamming the lid down.

McQueen squinted at him.

" You don't think we should disturb her right now?" he asked.

" Mrs. Marshall inherits," Ross said quietly.

McQueen got the message. Ross was telling him in so many words that Wicksteed's amusement park now hung on Mrs. Marshall's goodwill. If she was bothered with questions right now, she might not be inclined to part with the necessary funds.

McQueen cleared his throat, took off his Stetson and wiped his forehead. He looked like a man who has just avoided stepping on a rattle snake.

" Well, yes, I wouldn't want to disturb her at this time. The coroner will ask all the necessary questions. Yeah . . ." He got to his feet. " I'll send an ambulance up, Devery. You tell Mrs. Marshall to take it easy. Give her my condolences. The inquest will be in a couple of days. I'll let you know just when."

"Thank you, Sheriff." I got to my feet. "I'll tell Mrs. Marshall how considerate you have been."

He beamed.

"You do that, and tell her if there is anything worrying her to let me know. Let her know Wicksteed is behind her in her loss."

Ross left the room, carrying the bottle. When he had gone, McQueen offered his hand.

"Remember, Devery, Mrs. Marshall is now important. Put in a good word for us."

Shaking his hand, I said I would.

I watched them drive away, then went up the stairs to Beth's room.

She was standing in the doorway, waiting for me. I scarcely recognised her. She had changed into a dark grey frock with a white scarf at her throat. She had altered her hair style so it now came forward, covering the sides of her face. Her features seemed to have softened and her eyes were a little swollen. She looked like a woman who had suddenly lost her husband. How she had done it I had no idea, but she had done it.

I felt my fear drain away. First Ross, now this transformation. There was only one more hurdle . . . Bernstein, and she had said she could handle him. Looking at her, I was now sure she could.

"They've gone?"

"Yes. You're a millionairess now, Beth. The Sheriff didn't want to disturb you. He was scared stupid you might resent being disturbed and you wouldn't then finance their amusement park. We're nearly home. Everything now depends on Bernstein."

She stared thoughtfully at me. Again the remote look came into her eyes.

"No, it doesn't. Everything now depends on me."

The sound of a car pulling up made us stiffen.

"Here he is," I said.

She braced herself. The sad, lost look came into her eyes.

" Keep out of this," she said, and as the front door bell rang, she went down the stairs, crossed the hall and opened the front door.

*   *   *

Beth and Bernstein were still shut up together in the living-room when the ambulance arrived.

I went down and showed the two Interns where to find Marshall. They carried a stretcher into the garage and I took a walk around the garden. I was now almost certain that both of us were going to get away with murder. A lot still depended on how the coroner reacted, but I had an idea that Olson, Pinner and McQueen would cue him in. Beth was now important people to them.

But what really fazed me was the way Ross had acted. Maybe Pinner had got at him. There must be some good reason for him to have alerted McQueen to lay off, although, of course, the set-up, as Ross had said, was clear enough and the facts added up, but all the same his unexpected attitude when I was prepared for him to make trouble, baffled me.

I sat on the grass with my back to the house and thought again about Beth. I was more than uneasy about her, but, I kept telling myself, we were both in this together. Maybe, I thought, we could do a deal without me having to marry her, but I would have to handle this with kid gloves.

I heard the ambulance drive away, so I got to my feet and wandered back to the house. As I entered, I saw the living-room door was open and I could see Bernstein sitting alone, smoking a cigar. When he saw me, he beckoned.

I went in.

" Sit down." His face was stony. " You didn't do so well, did you?"

I sat down and looked directly at him.

" What was that again?"

" If you hadn't forgotten that whisky in the car, Frank would now be alive."

" You think so? I'll tell you something, Mr. Bernstein, you can't keep drink from a drunk. If not now, it would have been later."

He stared at me for a long moment, then shrugged.

" I'm taking care of Mrs. Marshall's affairs," he said. " What did Frank pay you?"

" Seven hundred."

He took out his wallet and thumbed out seven one hundred dollar bills which he put on the table.

" I want you to stick around here, Devery. I want you to look after the place, keep the garden right and take care of the sight-seers. There are bound to be ghouls who will come out here looking for souvenirs. Keep them out. I'm taking Mrs. Marshall to 'Frisco. My wife will take care of her until I can fix her affairs. You stick around until the house is sold. Is that okay?"

" Is she selling the house?" I asked, staring at him.

" Yeah. She doesn't want to live here any more and that's understandable. Yeah, she is selling the house."

" Well, okay, Mr. Bernstein. I'll take care of it."

He nodded.

" Right."

Beth appeared in the doorway. She was carrying a hold-all. Bernstein shot out of his chair and took the hold-all from her.

" Devery has agreed to stay on, Mrs. Marshall," he said, oil in his voice. " You go to my car. I won't be a minute."

I was staring at Beth. She looked broken. There was no other word for it. She held a sodden handkerchief with which she kept dabbing her eyes. She had probably dipped it in water before she had come down the stairs. She looked a shocked and sorrowing widow. As a performance she out-classed Hepburn.

She gave me a small, wan smile.

" Thank you for all you have done," she said, her voice

quavering. " Mr. Bernstein is so kind and understanding."

Bernstein and I watched her walk slowly to the front door. He picked up Marshall's locked brief-case.

" See you at the inquest," he said curtly, then nodding, he picked up the hold-all and went out to his car.

I stood in the doorway of the front door. Beth was huddling up in the passenger's seat, the sodden handkerchief held to her eyes. Bernstein gunned the engine and drove away.

That left me on my own.

From that moment, I had an instinctive feeling I was being edged out. It was a feeling I wouldn't accept, but it was there.

Beth had said she could handle Bernstein and she certainly had. I supposed our next meeting would be at the inquest. I would have to ask her where I could contact her. It would be dangerous for me to leave Wicksteed immediately after the inquest. I would have to stay around until the house was sold before moving to 'Frisco.

I spent a dreary, lonely day in the big, lonely house, trying to kill time. No one telephoned. No one came near. Finally, around 18.00, I got so sick of my own company, I drove into Wicksteed.

Parking, I went into Joe's saloon.

They were all there in a huddle : Pinner, Olson, Mason and a tall, lean bird I hadn't seen before. As soon as they saw me, they waved, and Pinner heaved himself out of his chair to cross the saloon to shake hands.

He signalled to Joe who brought a beer which he set on the table, nodding and smiling at me.

" Well, Keith, this is something, isn't it?" Pinner said. " Meet Luke Brewer." He waved to the tall, lean bird. " He's our coroner."

Brewer gave me a thin smile as he shook hands.

" What's been going on, Keith?" Pinner asked, leaning forward. " You've been right in the middle of it."

I sipped the beer, then sitting back, I gave them the photo. With the coroner listening, it was a perfect opportunity.

I told them what I had told McQueen. Sure McQueen had already given Brewer the facts, I was careful, but my story had more colour than the story I had given McQueen. I finished by saying Bernstein had taken Mrs. Marshall to 'Frisco and he was representing her.

This item of news brought Pinner, Olson and Mason stiff in their chairs.

" She's gone to 'Frisco?"

" That's it. The house is going to be sold." I paused. " My guess is Bernstein is tricky. He has a way with him. He was very close to Frank." I sat back and looked slowly at the four of them, then went on, " I did have a chance to talk to Mrs. Marshall about the amusement park idea before Frank died and she seemed interested. I think she could be persuaded now she has Frank's money, but this is my guess."

Pinner thought about this, then looked at Brewer.

" We wouldn't want to submit Mrs. Marshall to an ordeal at the inquest, would we, Luke?"

Brewer chewed his thumb nail as he got the message.

" There's no question of that. Mr. Devery's evidence will do. I don't think I'll even have to call Mrs. Marshall. It's a straight forward verdict: accidental death."

We all nodded.

And that was how it was.

The inquest went smoothly and fast. I was the principal witness: in fact the only witness. Brewer said it wasn't necessary to call Mrs. Marshall who sat at the back of the courtroom with Bernstein. He expressed sympathy of the court and sympathy of the citizens of Wicksteed. It was all over in thirty minutes.

Pinner shoved his way through the crowd to shake Beth's hand and murmur condolences. Bernstein whisked her away. I didn't have a chance to get near her. I didn't even catch her eye. She was pale, weepy and she looked nowhere . . . a great performance.

I watched Bernstein drive her away.

Pinner came up to me.

" What do you think, Keith?" he asked anxiously.

" If she doesn't play now, you can't blame yourself."

" But do you think she will?"

I had had enough of him and Wicksteed's greed.

" How the hell should I know?" I said and leaving him, I got in the Caddy and drove back to the big, lonely house.

The funeral was two days later. Practically all the citizens of Wicksteed turned up, but Beth didn't. Bernstein was there to represent her. He explained to Pinner who was leading the Wicksteed mob that Mrs. Marshall had collapsed. She had desperately wanted to be there, but her doctor had refused to let her attend.

Marshall's body, in an expensive coffin, was tucked away in the Wicksteed's burial ground next to his aunt's grave. I stood with the hypocritical mourners. Pinner stood by my side. Olson, Mason and the rest of them, all wearing black ties and looking mournful, flanked Bernstein who looked bored. The press took photographs.

After the burial, Pinner tried to talk to Bernstein, but he got nowhere. Bernstein bull-dozed his way through the crowd to me.

" You'll be hearing from me, Devery," he said. " Look after the house." Then he shoved his way to his car and drove off.

That seemed to be that.

Two days later, the local real estate agent came with a fat man and his fatter wife. They tramped over the house and decided to buy it as it stood. The price was right, and they were a couple who liked being on their own.

The following day while I was cooking a steak for lunch, the telephone bell rang.

It was Bernstein.

" I'm depositing seven hundred dollars in your bank, Devery," he said curtly. I could tell from the tone of his voice he had no time for me. " The house is sold. From now on, you're not needed. One other thing I'll get you to do : sell the

Caddy. Get the best for it and send the cheque to me."

"Okay, Mr. Bernstein." I paused, then said, "I would like to speak to Mrs. Marshall. Could you tell me where I can contact her?"

"She's right here. Hold on."

A long pause, then Beth said, "Hello, Keith?" Her voice sounded wooden and I could imagine the dead pan expression on her face.

"When can we meet?" I said, gripping the telephone receiver so tightly my knuckles turned white.

"Thank you for all you did for Frank." There was a slight shake in her voice. "I am very grateful. I hope you will be successful in finding another job," and she hung up.

Holding the receiver in my hand, I stared at it, feeling the cold dead finger creep up my spine, then I replaced the receiver.

Getting to my feet, I moved around the big room, feeling distrust and suspicion nibbling at my mind. After a minute or so, I told myself that she was playing the cards right. With Bernstein listening, she couldn't make a date with me—the hired hand. She was now a millionairess and important people. But how to contact her?

Bernstein had said she would be staying at his house. I had his home number. Sometime during the day, I would call and ask for her, then she would tell me her plans.

While waiting, I decided to do what Bernstein had told me to do : sell the Caddy. I had around a thousand dollars : three hundred which I had saved and the seven hundred Bernstein had given me. I was going to get another seven hundred from him in a day or so, so I wasn't short of cash.

I drove the Caddy to the Cadillac showroom, and after a lot of talk, got them to buy it back. I bought a VW second-hand at a knock down price. At least I was mobile. I had the cheque for the Caddy made out to Bernstein and mailed the cheque to him.

All this took time and I arrived back at the house around

17.00. Bernstein would still be at his office. Sweating a little, I called his home number.

A woman answered: " This is Mr. Bernstein's residence."

I drew in a long, slow breath.

" I would like to speak to Mrs. Frank Marshall."

" Will you hold on ?"

A long, long pause, then another woman's voice said, " Who is it ?" Certainly not Beth.

" I want to speak to Mrs. Marshall. This is Keith Devery."

" She is not here."

" It is important that I contact her." I tried to keep my voice steady. " Would you please give me her telephone number ?"

" You should ask Mr. Bernstein," and the line went dead.

For some moments, I sat hesitating. Should I wait ? Beth could telephone me at any moment, but I had a feeling she wouldn't. From the moment when she had left the house with Bernstein, I had had this vague suspicion she was walking out on me, and now the suspicion turned into frightening reality.

Snatching up the telephone receiver, I called Bernstein's office. After a delay, he came on the line.

" What is it, Devery ?" There was a hard, impatient snap in his voice.

" I want to speak to Mrs. Marshall," I said. " Where can I contact her ?"

" Have you sold the car ?"

" Yes. The cheque is in the mail. Where can I contact Mrs. Marshall ?"

" Now listen to me, Devery. You have been paid off. Mrs. Marshall isn't well. She told me she doesn't want to be bothered by you nor anyone else in Wicksteed. If there is anything you want to say, say it, and if it is important enough, I'll tell her. What is it ?"

Feeling cold and sick, and now realising that I had been taken for a sucker, I replaced the receiver.

I sat for some minutes, staring out of the window, then blood rushed to my head.

" Okay, Beth," I said aloud, spitting out the words. " Don't imagine you'll get away with this! I'll find you! You owe me half a million and I'm collecting it!"

I got to my feet and slammed my fists together.

" Make no mistake about that, you two-faced bitch! I'll find you!"

eight

I SPENT THE night in the bed on which Beth and I had made love so often. The wind moaned around the house and there were moments when I imagined I could hear Frank's dying fingers scratching on the garage door. It was probably the worst night I have ever lived through, although that first night when the cell door clanged shut, could have been worse, but not much worse.

I now had to accept the bitter fact that Beth had played me for a sucker. She had encouraged me to murder Frank; she had relied on my planning; she had gone along with everything I had said, and once Frank was dead, she had ditched me, knowing I couldn't expose her without exposing myself to a murder charge. Okay, she had been smart, but now, it was my turn to be smart. With a feeling of vicious fury, I told myself she wasn't going to get away with this. If it was the last thing I did, I would fix her.

Lying in the bed, I thought about her. I remembered our conversation which now seemed a long time ago.

I remembered saying to her : *What would you do if he died and you got his money?*

She had been lying, naked, by my side, and I could see her in my mind as clearly as if she were with me at this moment and I could hear her sigh as she said : *Do? I would go back to 'Frisco where I was born. A woman with a million dollars can have a ball in 'Frisco.*

If I could believe that then she would still be somewhere in 'Frisco, but 'Frisco was a big city. Hunting for her could be a slow, perhaps impossible task.

I moved restlessly as I thought. She was now worth a million. She wouldn't stay at some cheap hotel or motel. She would want to spend her money. She would install herself in some luxury apartment or some luxury hotel or even rent a house. I would have to be careful not to alert her I was hunting for her. To make inquiries could send her on the run. No: that wasn't the way to play it.

It wasn't until the sky turned grey and the first hint of the sun came through the big window that an idea occurred to me.

I remembered the big restaurant-cum-motel just outside 'Frisco and remembered her telling me that she once worked there. Then I remembered the chef . . . what was his name? Mario? Yes, Mario. He had been scared of her. Maybe if I handled him right, he could give me some information about her. I knew next to nothing about her except she had said she planned to live in 'Frisco, that she had been born there, that she had met Marshall at this restaurant. Before I began to hunt for her I had to get as much information about her as I could and Mario seemed a good bet.

I decided not to waste time. As soon as I had breakfast, I cleaned up, locked up the house, put the keys in an envelope addressed to the real estate agent, then getting in the VW, I drove down the dirt road to the 'Frisco highway, knowing I would never see that house again.

As I was about to edge out onto the highway, I saw Sheriff McQueen's car waiting to turn against the traffic. I felt my heart skip a beat. What was he doing here? Had he become suspicious?

McQueen was at the wheel and a young, fresh complexioned man, wearing police uniform sat at his side. Seeing me, McQueen waved, then as a gap appeared in the traffic, he swung the car and pulled up close to me.

I got out of my car and walked over to his, my heart thumping, my hands sweaty.

" Hi, Sheriff," I said. " You've just caught me. I'm pulling out."

" Meet Jack Allison, my new deputy," McQueen said, nodding to the man at his side.

" Hi," Allison said and gave me a friendly grin.

" So Ross finally got his transfer," I said for something to say.

" He's quit the force." McQueen shrugged. " Got himself a job with a Security company in 'Frisco." He grimaced. " Glad to see him go."

" I guess." A pause, then I said, " I'm going to 'Frisco myself. I'm hoping to find a job." I took the envelope containing the keys of the house from my pocket and offered it to him. " If you could give these keys to Mr. Curby, the real estate agent, I would be most obliged."

" I'll give them to him." He took the envelope and put it in his pocket. " So you're leaving. Why not stay in Wicksteed, Devery? You could do a lot worse. Bert was talking about you last night. He still wants you to be his partner."

I shook my head.

" I guess I'm footloose, Sheriff. I want to try my luck in a big city."

" Any news of Mrs. Marshall?"

" Not a thing. Mr. Bernstein is handling her affairs. He sacked me." I gave what I hoped was a rueful smile. " The house is sold. I guess that's it."

" Yeah. It doesn't look as if Mrs. Marshall will help with our scheme?"

" I wouldn't know, Sheriff. Joe could have a word with Mr. Bernstein."

" Yeah." He started his engine. " Well, okay, Devery. I wish you luck. Don't forget Bert still wants you as a partner. He thinks a lot of you."

" I won't forget."

I shook hands with him and then with Allison, then I got back into my car. I drove onto the highway, leaving them looking after me.

I arrived at the restaurant-cum-motel a little after 15.00. Parking the car, I walked into the restaurant, paused to look around, then picked a corner table near the bar. The lunch rush was over and the place was empty. After a minute or so, Mario came from the kitchen and wandered over to me. When he reached my table, he recognised me and his fat face lit up with a smile.

" It's Beth's friend," he said and offered his hand.

I shook hands with him.

" Have a beer with me if you're not busy," I said.

He laughed.

" Does it look as if I'm busy?" He waved to the empty room. " I won't get busy now for a couple of hours." He went away, poured two beers, returned and sat at the table. " Devery . . . that's the name, isn't it?"

" You have a good memory."

" Yeah. It helps to have a good memory in my business. People like to be recognised. Yeah . . . you were teaching her to drive . . . a joke." He laughed.

I stared directly at him.

" She made a good screw."

He nodded.

" I'm sure. I never got there myself, being happily married." He grimaced. " I don't need women like Beth."

" You heard about her husband . . . Frank Marshall?"

He sipped his beer, screwing up his eyes as he regarded me.

" What about him?"

" He's dead."

Putting down his beer, Mario crossed himself.

" God rest his soul. It will come to all of us." He drank some beer, then went on, " From what I've heard he wasn't much . . . a lush, wasn't he?"

" You can say that again."

" I heard he owned a big house. Did she get that?"

" That and some money."

He laughed and slapped his fat thigh.

" Trust Beth. She was always onto a winner. So she has the house and some money." He leaned forward as he asked, " How much?"

As if I would tell him.

" I wouldn't know . . . some money."

" Well, that's nice. Now she can keep her fancy cop in cigarettes and beer."

The cold dead finger crept up my spine. Somehow I managed to keep my face expressionless.

" Cop? What cop?"

" You wouldn't know him: a deputy at Wicksteed: one of those jerks who is always looking for trouble . . . name of Ross. She was crazy about him and I guess still is. On his day off, he would come here when she was running this joint. She would leave everything to me to handle and shack up with him in one of our cabins." He paused and winked at me. " The way you and she shacked up when she brought you here. Every week, he came and screwed her. To see her with him was something. She couldn't keep her eyes nor her hands off him. In my time, I've seen women besotted with men, but nothing like this. Well, if she had money now, he'll get it. He had a hook in her and, believe me, it's a hook that'll stay in."

I sat staring at him. What he had said hit me like a punch in the belly. I felt bile rush into my mouth. Getting up I ran to the men's room, somehow reached a loo, then threw up.

Ten minutes later, I got hold of myself. I washed my face, drank some water, then bracing myself, I returned to the restaurant. My heart beat was sluggish. I was sweating and my mind only half working.

Mario had finished his beer and stared at me as I joined him at the table.

" Something wrong?" he asked as I dropped into my chair.

153

" It's okay now. Something I ate last night. I had to throw up. Let's have a shot of whisky."

His face brightened.

" I don't often drink whisky, but why not?"

I had myself under control by the time he came back with a bottle of Old Roses and two shot glasses. He poured. We drank.

" What did you eat last night?" he asked sympathetically.

" Clams . . . never again."

" That's it. They are either right or they are poison. Are you okay now, Mr. Devery?"

I finished my drink, poured another and shoved the bottle his way.

" I'm fine. You were telling me about Ross. I met him. I once had a job in Wicksteed. I hear he has resigned from the police force and is in some security job here."

" Is that right?" Mario shrugged. " I wouldn't know."

" Have you seen Beth since I was last here?"

" No." He grimaced, sipped his drink, then added, " I'm not sorry. She always finds fault. Do you think she is in 'Frisco?"

" I know she is."

" Then maybe she'll look in." He finished his drink. " No skin off my nose if she doesn't."

" From what she told me, she always wanted to settle here." I poured him another drink.

" That's right. She was born here. Her father left her a little house on Orchard avenue. He called the house Apple Trees. She once told me there wasn't an apple on the place. She told me she had an offer to sell, but she wouldn't. She said the house was part of her background."

I had all I wanted to know. Finishing my drink, I dropped a five dollar bill on the table and stood up.

" Well, I guess I'm on my way," I said. " It's been nice talking to you."

He stared up at me.

" Is there something wrong?"

" Keep the change."

I walked out of the restaurant and to my car.

*   *   *

I booked into a cheap motel and shut myself in the small cabin. I needed to be on my own, to sit still and to think. I told the elderly reception clerk I had been driving all night and wanted to rest up for a while. He couldn't have been less interested. I asked him if he had a street guide of 'Frisco. He found one after searching through a drawer.

Shut up in the shabby air conditioned room, I lit a cigarette and took stock.

It was as if I had been blindfolded and now Mario's information had whipped off the blinder and I could see just what a sucker I had been.

With the cigarette burning between my fingers, I thought back. I recalled the first time I had met Ross. I could see him clearly : tall, thin, young—around twenty-nine—small hard cop eyes and a thin mouth. Beth's lover! A man, according to Mario, with whom Beth was besotted. By sheer chance he had investigated me and had found I had been in jail. He must have discussed me with Beth. I was a stranger in town with a criminal record. To them, I must have seemed a gift from the gods to be used as their cat's paw. Ross had been at the railroad station when Marshall had arrived, drunk. I was sure now this had been a deliberate set-up. I had fallen for it by driving Marshall home and he had fallen for it by hiring me to act as his chauffeur. Probably Beth had persuaded him he must have someone to drive him. The rest had been too easy. All she had to do was to get me on the bed. The rest of the grave I had dug for myself. Then I remembered the time when I had driven Marshall back from 'Frisco and had found Ross with Beth. He had probably been screwing her, thinking Marshall would be away for three or four days. They must have had a hell of a fright, but they had played it so cool, they had fooled me. I now could understand why Ross had said Marshall's death was an open and shut case. The last thing either of them would want was a murder investigation and McQueen and Luke Brewer had fallen for it.

I moved restlessly.

Both of them had certainly played it smart, landing me with a murder and no money. They were probably laughing their heads off that they had found such a sucker.

Well, she had got the money and she had got her boy-friend, but she and Ross still had me, although right now they wouldn't know that.

Picking up the street guide I located Orchard avenue. There was just a chance she was there with him. After all, I reasoned, she couldn't have got the money just yet although Bernstein would arrange credit for her, but there was still a chance she was there.

If I found her what was I going to do?

I thought about this. It presented a problem. It would be useless to corner her and demand my share of the money. She would only laugh at me. Suppose I threatened to tell Bernstein the whole story? That wouldn't get me anywhere except a long term in jail, even if she got one too, but with her money and Bernstein working for her the chances of her drawing a murder rap were remote. It would be my word against hers and I would have to admit it had been my plan and I had actually murdered Marshall. She could swear she hadn't known a thing about it, and there was no proof that she had.

After more thinking, I was sure that trying to bluff her would only land me in trouble. I would have to find some way to get the money out of her, and that I was determined to do.

Then I remembered what Mario had said: *a deputy at Wicksteed. She was crazy about him and I guess, still is. To see her with him was something. She couldn't keep her eyes nor her hands off him. He had a hook in her and, believe me, it's a hook that will stay in.*

If this were true, and I had to make sure it was true, then Ross could give me the chance of getting the money from her.

It came down to this: was Ross's life worth five hundred thousand dollars to her? If it wasn't then I would have to think again, but if it was, the money was as good as mine.

I remained in the motel cabin until dusk, then I went over to the café and had a hot dog and a coffee. There were very few people in the café and none of them paid any attention to me.

Orchard avenue was tucked away off one of the climbing hills south-west of the city. I found it with some difficulty, having to stop and ask a couple of times. As soon as I saw the street sign, I found parking and leaving the VW, I walked down the long street with wooden bungalow style houses either side. Each house had a name, but I didn't find *Apple Trees*. The street was some two hundred yards long so I crossed and started down the other side.

Half-way down I saw a fat woman leaning on a gate, smoking a cigarette and taking the night air. As I walked by her, she said, " You looking for someone, mister? I see you looking."

The street lighting wasn't much but I could just make out a fat, friendly looking face. She was wearing a shapeless dress and she looked lonely. I had my back to the light so she couldn't make much of me.

" Good evening," I said. " Yes, I was looking for a house."

She nodded.

" I guessed you were. These house names are darned stupid. Why not numbers? Maybe I can help you."

My mind worked swiftly. Was this dangerous? She could be a friend of Beth's, but looking at her, I doubted it.

" Apple Trees," I said. " I hear it is up for rent. I'm looking for a place for my wife and kids."

She sucked smoke down, coughed, then thumped her floppy bosom.

" I shouldn't smoke, but I can't give it up—no will power."

157

She dropped her cigarette butt on the grass and put her foot on it. " Apple Trees?" She gave a snort. " You'd never find it unless you were told. Top of the road, down a narrow lane between two houses and it's right at the back, but don't waste your time, mister. It's not for rent. *She* moved back a couple of days ago."

The way she emphasised ' she ' alerted me. Disapproval oozed from her.

" These estate agents!" I made a gesture of disgust. " They told me the place was for rent."

" She's never rented it." The fat woman shook her head. " It's stood empty for three years. Then suddenly she arrives with her fancy man . . . a couple of days ago."

My heart skipped a beat.

Keeping my voice steady, I said, " Maybe she's getting it ready to rent."

" I wouldn't bet on it." She lit another cigarette. " This is a respectable street, mister. None of us living here need a couple like them shacking up together. It's disgraceful!"

" At the end of the road? While I'm here, I may as well ask her. She could be thinking of renting."

" You got kids, mister?"

" A boy and a girl," I lied.

" Then you go along and talk to her. We could do with a few kids on this street. We're all old people . . . good for nothing. I'd rather have kids here than her and her fancy man."

" I can but ask. Thanks for your help."

" I wish you luck. What did you say your name was?"

" Lucas . . . Harry Lucas."

" I'm Emma Brody. If you get fixed up tell your wife to drop in and see me." Nodding, she plodded back to her house.

I waited until she had shut the front door, then turning, I walked back to the end of the road. I found a narrow dirt road between two bungalows as she had said. The road was just wide enough between the hedges of the two bungalows to take a car. For a long moment I hesitated. If I walked up there and Beth or Ross or both of them came driving down, I would be trapped, but I didn't hesitate for long. I went up the road fast, half running. There was no street lighting but the road was moon-lit. It curved suddenly and I saw the bungalow set in a small garden and there was a lighted sign on the gate: *Apple Trees.*

Light showed behind red curtains and a TV set was blasting. There was a car port. I could see a car which looked like a convertible two-seater parked there.

I stood at the gate looking at the bungalow. It was L-shaped. Probably it had three bedrooms and a big living-room. As I stood there I saw a shadow cross the curtains. I would know that thin outline anywhere . . . Beth!

I lifted the gate latch and pushing the gate open I walked across the grass to the bungalow. The windows were open and some pop singer was yelling his head off.

I moved close to the window and waited.

The yelling went on for some ten minutes, then suddenly the set was snapped off.

" If I hear any more of this crap I'll go out of my mind!"

The sound of Ross's snarling voice made me stiffen.

" Try another station, darling," Beth said. She had never called me that. " The fights will be on in half an hour."

" Who the hell cares about those bums?" Ross demanded. " Hell! I'm getting sick of living in this crummy hole. All these old fossils staring at us and gossiping. I want out!"

" But we must wait, darling. I've told you that. The money won't come to me for another two weeks."

" Two weeks! I'm not staying here for two weeks! You'll be getting the money for the house, won't you? Let's take an apartment . . . something with class."

" Don't you really like it here, honey? I was born here. I look on it as my real and only home." There was a pleading note in her voice.

" Oh God! Don't start that again!" He sounded savage.

" We're at last in the money! We're not going to live in a two bit bungalow. You talk to that crum Bernstein. Tell him you want action!"

" He mustn't know about you yet, darling. He's smart. I don't want him to get ideas."

" So, okay, he's smart, but tell him you want a big advance, then let's get out of 'Frisco. We could go to Miami and lose ourselves. Once we get the money, we get lost."

" I've always wanted to settle in 'Frisco."

" Forget it! You'll love Miami and we're away from gossip."

" All right, honey, anything you say."

" That's it . . . anything I say. Come here."

I stepped back and moved quietly back to the gate.

A revealing conversation. It told me she was hooked and that was all I wanted to know. It also told me she wouldn't have the money for another two weeks. I could wait. In the meantime I would have to buy a gun.

*　　　*　　　*

Having spent a restless night at the motel and eaten a badly cooked breakfast, I called my bank at Wicksteed and checked that Bernstein had deposited the $700 he owed me to my credit. He had. I told the clerk to have the amount credited to the Chase National branch which was right by the motel. He said he would do it right away. I then went across to the Chase National and opened an account with them, telling them of the deposit on the way.

I was now worth $1700 and that would be plenty for the time being. I then drove down town. After looking around, I went into a big pawnshop and told the clerk I wanted to buy a hand gun.

There was no problem about that. He offered a Smith & Wesson, a Browning .32 and a Mauser 7.63. I chose the Mauser because it looked impressive and was a top class engineering job with a detachable shoulder holster and it also looked menacing. He sold me a box of twenty-five slugs. Then regarding me, he said I would need a police permit. I got the idea he was registering my face in his mind. That I had to expect. I said I'd go around to the station house right away. I gave him a fictitious name and address, signed a form and that was that.

During my service in Vietnam I had learned how to handle firearms. The Mauser held no mysteries for me.

Putting the gun in my glove compartment, I then drove out towards Orchard avenue. On the way up the previous night I had spotted a real estate agent's office. Reaching it, I parked and walked into a small office where a bald, fat man sat behind a shabby desk, twiddling his thumbs and staring into space. He showed me yellow teeth, got up, waved me to a chair and asked what he could do for me.

I said I was interested in buying or renting a property on Orchard avenue. He looked sad, shook his head and said no houses on Orchard avenue were available, but he had some nice properties . . .

I interrupted him, saying I fancied Orchard avenue and that's where I wanted a house.

" Well, it depends on how long you can wait. They are old people up there and they pass on from time to time. You never know. An old lady died last year and the house was snapped up by another old lady. It is a matter of time."

" I can wait," I said. " I've still to sell my house in L.A. Right now I have a job here. Is there a chance of getting a furnished room on Orchard avenue while I wait?"

He found a pin behind his coat lapel and began to explore his yellow teeth while he thought.

" Maybe," he said finally. " Mrs. Emma Brody might take in a lodger. I've known her for years. She lost her husband not so long ago. She might be interested. Why not try her?"

" You wouldn't have a plan of the estate, would you?"

He dug into a file and gave me a plan. I asked him to locate Mrs. Brody's house. He marked it with a pencil.

" What's this house here?" I asked, pointing to *Apple Trees*.

" Not for sale. I've tried dozens of times to get the owner to part: no soap."

I was examining the plan. I could see from Mrs. Brody's rear windows, she would have a direct view of Beth's place.

It would seem the cards were falling my way. I thanked him, said I would call on Mrs. Brody and should I mention his name? He shook his head sadly, said he just wanted to be helpful. Rentals were more bother than they were worth.

After shaking hands with him, I left him twiddling his thumbs and drove up to Orchard avenue. I parked outside Mrs. Brody's house and rang the door bell.

She came to the door, a cigarette dangling from her lips.

I explained who I was and she recognised me. Her fat, friendly face lit up.

" Apple Trees isn't for rent," I said, " but the agent said property does come up for sale from time to time and I can wait. I like it here. He said you might have a room to rent. I'm working on a computer system and need quiet. Would you consider renting me a room?"

Again there was no problem. She wanted me to have the best bedroom overlooking the street, but I said I wanted quiet, so she showed me the back bedroom which was small, but comfortably furnished. I looked out of the window: a little more than a hundred yards away, I could see *Apple Trees*.

We made terms and I said I would move in that afternoon. She said if I wanted meals she would be happy to oblige. As I intended to keep a twenty-four hour watch on the bungalow I wouldn't want to go out so I arranged with her to supply two simple meals a day.

Leaving her, I drove back to the motel, checked out, then going to another pawnshop, I bought a pair of powerful field glasses and a portable typewriter. Then from a nearby store I bought a pack of typing paper and a couple of notebooks. I wanted to look convincing when Mrs. Brody cleaned my room.

I had lunch and then moved into my room. Mrs. Brody

gave me a key. She seemed inclined to gossip, but I cut her short, saying I had to start work right away.

" If you want to see some TV while you're here, you come down. I like a bit of company."

I thanked her and went up to the room, shut and locked the door, pulled up a chair and getting out the field glasses, I focussed them on *Apple Trees.*

So began a four day and half the night's vigil. After three days, I got the pattern of the way Beth and Ross lived.

Around ten o'clock, Ross went off in the car. Soon after eleven, Beth, carrying a shopping bag, left the house and went away on a motor-scooter. She got back around 12.45. Ross didn't show up until 18.00. From time to time I got a good view of them at the window. They didn't go out in the evening, but settled down to watching the tube.

It seemed to me a dull kind of life considering the money she was worth until I realised they were afraid to be seen together in the city. They could run into Bernstein who was sharp enough to recognise Ross, having seen him at the inquest and at the funeral.

Mrs. Brody provided adequate meals. I did a little typing to convince her I was working. Fortunately, she was often out visiting neighbours. On the fourth morning, as she was cleaning my room, she said I should go out and get some fresh air.

I said my work was urgent and I was a night bird.

" I take a walk when you are in bed. You don't have to worry about me."

For the next six days, I watched, and finally, I was satisfied that Beth was always alone from 13.00 to 18.00. I decided it was time to make my first move.

So that afternoon, just after 14.00, I went to my parked VW, got the Mauser from the glove compartment, stuck it in my waist band and then wandered up the street and up the dirt road to *Apple Trees.*

Beth was in the garden, on her knees, weeding the rose bed.

I approached her silently over the grass and she wasn't aware of me until my long shadow fell before her.

She remained motionless for a brief moment, then quickly looked over her shoulder.

We looked at each other and I wondered how I could have ever been so infatuated with her. The sight of her hard, mask-like face, her remote eyes and the hard set of her mouth now sickened me.

" Hello, Beth," I said quietly. " Remember me?"

She stood up slowly and faced me. I had given her a hell of a shock, but it scarcely showed.

" What do you want?" Her voice hard and cold.

" Let's go inside and talk," I said.

" Get out!" She spat the words at me.

" Just a short talk, Beth. It would be better for you and for Ross."

I saw her flinch. So Mario had been right. She was still hooked.

" I've nothing to say to you." There was no conviction in her voice. " Get out!"

I started towards the bungalow, and after hesitating, she came after me. We went inside and I found my way into the big living-room. It was a nice room, well furnished and homely.

As she moved past me, I closed the door and leaned against it.

" I want my half share of Frank's money," I said.

Her hands closed into fists and her dark eyes glittered.

" Try and get it!"

" I said I would keep it short, so I'll keep it short." I pulled the Mauser from my belt and showed it to her.

Her eyes widened and she took a step back.

" Relax, Beth. You don't have to worry about yourself. This gun has a magazine of ten bullets. Not one of them is intended for you, but all ten of them are reserved for Ross unless you part with five hundred thousand dollars."

Her mouth twitched.

" You get nothing from me, you cheap bluffer!"

" Don't make that mistake, Beth. I'm not bluffing. A half a million isn't something I bluff about. Having killed one man, another means nothing to me. I'm telling you, unless I get my share by the end of the month, Ross will get ten slugs in his gut. There's nothing to stop me. You can't go to the police for protection. They would ask questions and that's something you don't want. It could take me a little time to set him up, but I'll get him and there's nothing you nor he can do about it. I know his routine. I'm having him watched. If he tries to skip, I'll go after him. You either part with my share or he dies. Please yourself. I've been watching you two for two days. I know he wants you to go with him to Miami. You would be surprised how much I do know about you both. I'll give you to the end of this week, then I'll telephone you. You either say yes or no. That's up to you. If you say yes, I'll arrange how you pay me the money. If you say no, then Ross is as good as dead with his guts blown to hell."

Without looking at her, I opened the door, stepped out into the hall, then walked without hurrying down the garden path, onto the dirt road and back to Mrs. Brody's house.

Now it was up to her and as sure as I was feeling the hot sun on my back, I would kill Ross if she didn't play.

*   *   *

Back in my room, I sat down, lit a cigarette, and took stock.

Beth now knew she was no longer dealing with a sucker. I had put my cards on the table: pay up or you lose your boy-friend. Knowing her, I was sure she wouldn't part with five hundred thousand dollars without a fight. But what would she do?

I tried to put myself in her place and to think as she must be thinking now. Would she tell Ross? If she did, how would Ross react? He was a tough, ex-cop, but he could have a yellow streak. He couldn't run to the 'Frisco cops to help him.

They would want to know what it was all about and he was in no position to answer probing questions.

After some thought, it seemed to me, Beth and he had only two alternatives : to pay up or to kill me before I killed him.

If Ross was a killer, why hadn't he murdered Marshall instead of dragging me into the act as their cat's paw? It was possible he hadn't the guts to kill, but I knew she had. Still, I warned myself, I mustn't underestimate Ross. He could turn killer to keep that money.

I had told her I was having him watched. Would they believe that? The fact that I had told her I knew they were planning to go to Miami must have made an impact. Suppose they decided to make a run for it . . . leave in the middle of the night and vanish? Maybe they would decide the risk was too great. They couldn't be sure I wasn't watching and Ross could walk into a bullet.

Suppose Ross decided to hunt for me? They might guess I was somewhere on this estate. I was pretty sure Mrs. Brody had told her neighbours she had a lodger. Was Ross in the position to make inquiries? I thought not. According to Mrs. Brody and what he had said, no one on the estate approved of Beth nor of Ross. No one was friendly with them, but there were people like the milkman, the postman and the newsboy. Mrs. Brody might talk to them and Ross, with his police training, might learn from them about Mrs. Brody's new lodger.

If they guessed I was holed up in the small back room, watching them, what could they do about it? Would Ross, with a gun, break in one night? He just might, but I had a gun too, and he now knew it. Would he have the guts? If he chickened out, how about Beth? She might.

Getting up, I examined the door of my bedroom. It was solid and had an old fashioned mortice lock. Neither Beth nor Ross could take me by surprise and if they tried to, it would end in a shoot out with Mrs. Brody screaming for the police. I decided as long as I remained in the room, I was safe. I had another five days to the end of the week. I could stay in this room for five days with no sweat.

Because I was sure there would be no action until Ross returned at 18.00, I lay on the bed and took a nap. For all I knew I might have to sit up all the night.

I didn't wake up until Mrs. Brody came tapping on the door with my dinner at 19.15.

Cursing myself for over sleeping, I let Mrs. Brody in.

" I guess I was taking a nap," I said as she put down the tray.

" Just cold cuts tonight, but there's a nice salad," she said. " I'm going to the movies."

" That's fine. Have a good time."

" If you want to watch TV, you're welcome."

" Not tonight, thanks."

When she had gone, I went over to the window and took up the field glasses. Although it was still light, the red curtains were drawn. I would have given a lot to know what was going on in that big comfortable room. Had Beth told him?

I hurriedly ate the meal. As I finished I heard the front door slam. I sat down and watched the red curtains. When it grew dark, the lights behind the curtains went on. I watched for the next three hours, but nothing happened. Around 22.30, I heard Mrs. Brody come in and go to her room. I stayed watching *Apple Trees* until the lights went out in the living-room and came up in one of the bedrooms.

Then unlocking my door, I went silently down to the living-room. I had already got Beth's telephone number from the book and I dialled the number.

There was a long delay, then she said, " Who is it?"

" I'm watching the end of your lane, Beth," I said. " Sleep well," and I hung up.

If that didn't stick, nothing would, so I returned to my room and went to bed.

The pattern of their lives changed the following morning. Ross didn't leave the bungalow as usual at ten o'clock. So she had told him! Nor did she leave to go shopping and the red curtains remained drawn. The newsboy arrived and tossed a paper on their porch, but neither of them came out to collect it.

A sign of nerves?

I thought so . . . a good sign for me.

I found it a strain to spend the whole day watching, but I watched. There was no sign of either of them. I had plenty of time to think and I decided to make things tricky for them if they decided to bolt.

So around one in the morning, when I was sure Mrs. Brody was asleep, I slipped out of the house and made my way to *Apple Trees*.

The bungalow was in darkness, but I took my time approaching it. I had had a lot of experience in jungle fighting and I knew how to approach a hostile objective silently and without being seen.

I reached the car port. The car door was unlocked. I opened the hood. Then using my flashlight, I removed the distributor head which I dropped into my pocket. I closed the hood, then returned the way I had come.

There would now be no quick packing and bolting, I thought, and undressing I got into bed.

The following day Beth went off on the motor-scooter, but Ross didn't show nor were the red curtains drawn back. I was beginning to think I had him scared, but I was taking no chances. I kept my bedroom door locked and kept a constant vigil at the window.

Beth got back in under an hour.

Two more days to go.

When Mrs. Brody had gone out, I went into her living-room and called Beth's number.

When she answered, I said, " If lover boy wants a slug in his guts, tell him to come looking for me tonight at the end of the lane. I'll be waiting," and I hung up.

I was a great believer in a war of nerves.

168

I maintained my watch on the bungalow for the rest of the evening, but no one showed.

After dinner, I typed a message :

Only two more days, Beth. It is up to you.

Around midnight when the lights in the living-room of *Apple Trees* were still on and Mrs. Brody was in bed, I left the house and made a cautious way to the bungalow. On the way there, I found a heavy stone. I tied my note to the stone with a piece of string I had brought with me.

I approached the bungalow. There was no sound from the television set and the windows were closed.

When I was close enough, I stood up and heaved the stone at the middle window of the living-room. The glass smashed and the stone brushed by the flimsy red curtain and thumped on the floor.

The Mauser in my hand, I dropped flat and waited.

There was a long pause, then the lights went out.

I waited.

Here was the test. Would Ross show?

Nothing happened. I lay on the grass and waited. I waited for twenty minutes. No sound came from the bungalow : no lights showed.

Ross wasn't coming out for a High Noon shoot up.

Gutless?

I edged my way back across the grass, then when I reached the dirt road, I stood up and walked back to my room.

nine

ONE MORE day, I thought as I waited for Mrs. Brody to bring my breakfast. The set-up looked good to me. I had turned the screw last night and Ross hadn't accepted the challenge. Had I been in his place, I knew that stone and the broken window would have been such a challenge, I would have come out fighting . . . but not Ross.

Yes, it looked good to me.

As Mrs. Brody set down the tray, she said, " I have to go out, Mr. Lucas. A neighbour of mine has been taken ill. Would you mind if lunch is late : I won't get back before two o'clock."

" Suppose you leave me a sandwich? Then you needn't worry to hurry back."

She beamed.

" Thank you. That's real considerate. I'll leave it in the kitchen."

After breakfast, I went to the window and watched. A few minutes after nine o'clock, Beth appeared and went to the car. Even from this distance I could hear the engine growling as she tried to start it. Finally, she gave up and went back to the bungalow. I guessed she was telling Ross the car had broken down. Would he show?

I waited. Some fifteen minutes later, Beth appeared and drove off on her motor-scooter.

So it would seem Ross was still too scared to come out in the open.

Beth hadn't been gone more than three minutes when I heard the telephone bell ringing in the living-room. I went to my door, unlocked and opened it.

I heard Mrs. Brody say, " Hello?"

There was a pause, then she said, " Who? No one of that name here ... what name again? Devery? No." A long pause, then she said, " There's a Mr. Lucas here." Another pause. " Yes, that's right : he's staying here." Another pause. " Hold it. I'll ask him."

So Ross, the ex-cop, had found me. I wasn't surprised nor alarmed. I went out onto the passage as Mrs. Brody, dressed to go out, came from the living-room.

" There's a man asking for you, Mr. Lucas. I must go : I'm late already."

" Thanks. I hope your friend isn't too bad."

I watched her leave, then I went into the living-room and picked up the telephone receiver.

" Yes?"

" Is that you, Devery?" Ross's voice sounded shaky.

" Suppose it is?"

" I've got to talk to you!"

" I don't need to talk to you, Ross. I talk only to Beth."

" Listen ... I've got to talk to you! She won't be back for an hour. This is my chance. I want to come to you."

A voice can convey a lot of things. His voice conveyed fear.

" Okay, Ross. I don't know how good a shot you are, but I'm good. So if you want a shoot out, come and have one."

" I haven't got a gun! I swear I haven't a gun!" He was almost babbling.

He was either telling the truth or he was a great con man.

" Here's what you do, Ross. Come to the house. The front door will be open. Come in, walk down the passage and enter the third room on the left. I'll be waiting with a gun," and I hung up.

I went to the window and watched. Two minutes later, Ross appeared. He was wearing a sweat shirt and cotton slacks. I put the field glasses on him. I couldn't see any bulge made by a hidden gun. I lifted the glasses and examined his face. As he walked towards me, half running, half walking, his face became bigger and bigger in the lenses of the glasses. I scarcely recognised him from the hard, tough cop who had whistled to me when first we had met. This was a wreck of a man: white face, dark rings of exhaustion under his eyes and a slack twitching mouth.

It seemed my war of nerves had reduced him to pulp.

I left the front door open and my bedroom door. Then I went into Mrs. Brody's bedroom, Mauser in hand and half shut the door. I was taking no chances.

After five minutes or so, I heard him come in. He shut the front door.

" Devery? " There was a quaver in his voice.

I waited.

He walked slowly down the passage and stopped at my door as I moved onto the passage.

" Stay right there, Ross, " I said, a snap in my voice.

He froze.

I moved up to him, dug the barrel of the Mauser into his spine and ran my hand over his body. Satisfied he wasn't carrying a gun, I shoved him into my room.

He walked unsteadily to the middle of the room and stopped. He didn't turn.

" I'm quitting, Devery, " he said. " You've got no quarrel with me. I've had enough. "

I moved away from him.

" Sit down. "

He went to an armchair and flopped into it. I sat on the bed, pointing the Mauser at him.

We looked at each other. This was no con trick. Here was a frightened, sweating creep who was only thinking of himself.

I put the gun down beside me and took out a pack of

cigarettes, lit one, then tossed the pack to him. He fumbled the catch, let the pack fall to the floor, scrabbled for it, then with a shaking hand, lit up.

"Go ahead, Ross," I said. "Talk."

"She's crazy!" he blurted out. "I can't take any more of her! I've been shut up with her now for days. She's out of her mind! She's gone downtown to buy a gun! She wants me to come out here and kill you!"

I regarded him, feeling only contempt.

"Don't you want to kill me, Ross? Think of all that money you'll have if I'm dead."

"Money?" His voice turned shrill. "I don't give a damn about money now!" He slammed his fists together. "I want out! All her talk! She drives me crazy! Listen, Devery, I swear I didn't know she was planning to murder her husband! I swear it! You've got to believe me! The moment I met her I knew she was a nutter, but she was a good screw. I couldn't keep away from her. I did tell her about your record, but I didn't know what she was planning. I swear it, Devery! I don't go along with murder. Not for all the money in the world! When she told me what you and she had done . . . killing Marshall, I flipped my lid. I wanted out, but she showed me how she could involve me. She's crazy about me, but to me, she's just a lay." He paused and looked wildly around the room. "You've got to believe me. I want out but she said if I make a move you'll shoot me! I don't want to die! I don't want her nor her money . . . I want out!"

"You should have thought of that before," I said to keep him talking.

"Thought?" He clutched his head. "I've done nothing else but think! I want out!"

"Oh, shut up! You knew what she was planning. You wanted the money. You covered up for her. An open and shut case. Remember? It was you who persuaded McQueen to leave her alone. It was you who got me to play killer while you stood on the sidelines, waiting to pick up the money. The problem with you is you're yellow. So long as you felt safe, waiting to pick up the money, you were happy, but when Beth told you I was gunning for you, you couldn't take it. Now listen to me : unless Beth agrees to give me five hundred thousand dollars, you're dead." I picked up the Mauser. " There are ten slugs in this gun. They are all for you. You either talk Beth into playing or else . . . and I'm not bluffing."

His face turned grey.

" I can't talk her into it! I tell you . . . she's out of her head!"

" Then it's too bad for you." I stood up. " Get out!"

" Devery . . ." He was shaking. " What have I done to you? Give me a break! Let me get away. I'll go now!"

" Haven't you got the message, Ross? Without you, I'd never get the money from her. You make one false move and you're dead. Now get out!"

He got unsteadily to his feet. He stared at me, started to say something, then stopped.

" Beat it!" I barked.

He went, his head down, his shoulders hunched, shaking.

Lack of moral fibre? Yellow through and through.

*   *   *

I was at the window when Beth arrived back on the motor-scooter. She was carrying a shopping bag and I wondered if she had bought the gun. I was pretty sure Ross wouldn't have the guts to come here, but she could. She wouldn't come until it was dark. I would have to sit up all night. I went into the kitchen, found the pack of sandwiches Mrs. Brody had left and returned to my room. I locked the door, ate the sandwiches, then stretched out on the bed.

The idea of Beth coming here with a gun was a joke. I was sure she had never handled a gun in her life . . . so let her come! I was confident I could handle her. I went to sleep.

When Mrs. Brody brought me my dinner, I had been up

for over an hour. There had been no activity at *Apple Trees* and I didn't expect any until it was dark.

I inquired after Mrs. Brody's friend and was told she was better. Mrs. Brody had brought the evening newspaper.

" You've been so busy, Mr. Lucas, I do believe you haven't heard all the news . . . not that it makes happy reading. I've finished it. I thought you would like it."

I thanked her. She was right. I had forgotten the world, outside this room and inside *Apple Trees* existed, but I wasn't interested. I ate the dinner, then as it was still light, I sat down by the window and glanced through the paper. When I reached the financial page, I received a shock. Charrington and Pittsburgh steel corporations had merged! There was a photo of Jack Sonson of Charrington steel looking smug. The report said that after six years of secret negotiations, Sonson had finally persuaded Pittsburgh to take over. The Charrington shares had trebled overnight.

So drunk Marshall had been right and I had been wrong! This was the bitterest blow I had ever experienced. Had I waited before murdering him and let the deal go through both Beth and I would now be worth three million instead of less than one.

I sat there, absorbing this frustrating and bitter blow. Too late! With me, it seemed it was always to be too goddamn late! But at least I would get five hundred thousand out of her, but how hollow that sounded to a million and a half!

I remained by the window, watching *Apple Trees* until dark. I could hear the TV set in the living-room. Mrs. Brody was occupied. Taking the Mauser and leaving my light on, I silently left the house and made my way to *Apple Trees*. Three quarters of the way up the dirt road there was a clump of shrubs and trees. I paused there. I could see Beth's bungalow clearly so I got behind the shrubs, nursing the Mauser and prepared for a long wait. I could see the lights were on behind the red curtains in the living-room and I wondered what was going on. I was sure Beth would get no help from Ross.

When fighting in the Vietnamese jungles, I had seen men go to pieces. Ross had gone to pieces and no amount of threats or persuasion from her would stiffen his broken spine.

So Beth would have to make up her mind either to handle me herself or pay up. One thing I was sure of : she was no quitter . . . so I had to be prepared for her to do something desperate.

Around 23.30, I heard her coming down the road.

Trained in jungle warfare, to me, her cautious approach was pathetic. She had no idea how to move silently. She kicked stones, moved too fast, brushed against brambles and did everything I had been trained not to do.

It was moonless and dark, but I had been sitting there for three hours and my eyes were now accustomed to the dark. I saw her coming. She was wearing black, but her white face was a complete give away.

I got into a crouching position and waited. Then as she passed me, I jumped her. My hands gripped her arms, my knees slamming into her back. She went down with a stifled scream. It took a moment to wrest the gun out of her hands, then still kneeling on her, I said, " Not even a good try, Beth."

She lay flat and still.

I shifted off her and stood, up moving away from her.

" You have until tomorrow," I said.

Slowly, she got to her feet and faced me.

" Don't go buying another gun," I said. " You are not using your head. You would never get away with killing me. I've left a letter with my bank. It tells the whole story. So don't try any more of this nonsense. Pay up or I'll put ten slugs into lover boy."

She just stood there, motionless and silent. I wish there had been enough light to see her face. All I could see was a white blob.

Then moving around her, I started back to Mrs. Brody's bungalow. The gun I had taken from her wasn't much : a .22. It could cause damage at close range, but useless at a distance.

Instinct, born in the jungle, alerted me to look back. She was coming at me like a charging wild cat. Her arm upraised.

Many Viets had come at me this way. It was too easy. I waited until she was almost on me, then dropped on hands and knees as the knife she was holding slashed harmlessly. Her knees thudded against my shoulder and she went flying, landing with a thud, face down, on the road.

Going over to her, I took the knife from her.

" You have guts, Beth," I said, and meant it. " You are way out of my class. Go back to that gutless, yellow cop and tell him how brave you are."

Holding the knife and the gun, I continued on down the dirt road, leaving her lying there.

*   *   *

When Mrs. Brody brought my breakfast, she said she had to spend the day with her sick friend.

" She needs cheering up, Mr. Lucas and I'm good at cheering people up. I've left you some cold chicken and ham in the refrig, and tonight, I'll give you a pot roast."

I told her not to worry. I would be busy all the morning and the cold chicken would be fine.

She left the house soon after 09.00. I now had the place to myself.

Today was the day.

Beth had made her try and had failed. Now it was my turn. Pay up or else! While eating my breakfast, I thought about her and Ross and wondered what they were saying to each other. Was she hatching up a new scheme to get rid of me? But time had run out for her. I was now confident she would pay up.

After breakfast, I sat at the table and typed out instructions to her as to how she was to pay the money to me. Five hundred thousand was a lump and I would have to spread it to avoid awkward questions. A hundred thousand could go to the Chase

National branch who already had my account. Another hundred thousand could go to Wicksteed. The rest of the money could go to the American Fidelity Bank in Los Angeles where I once had an account.

Around 10.00, I phoned Beth.

When she answered, I said, " Today is the day, Beth. What's the answer . . . yes or no?"

There was a pause, then she said in her cold, flat voice, " I want to talk to you."

" What's there to talk about? It's either yes or no. What is it?"

" Bernstein says the probate is delayed. I won't get the money for at least another month."

" Quit stalling! You can get credit. Tell Bernstein you must have five hundred thousand dollars by the end of the week. He'll fix it."

There was another long pause, then she said, " He'll want to know why. What can I tell him?"

I felt a surge of triumph run through me.

" So the answer is yes?"

" I must talk to you. This is something I can't discuss over the telephone."

" Is it yes or no?" I barked.

" I'm coming to see you now," and she hung up.

Another trick?

I went to the window and focussed the field glasses on *Apple Trees*. She appeared. She was wearing a tight-fitting dress and carried no handbag. Her hands were in sight. She wasn't carrying a gun nor a knife. I left the front door open and then retreated to my room. I trusted her the way I would trust a rattlesnake. Holding the Mauser by my side, I waited.

After a while, I heard her at the door.

" Come on in, Beth," I called.

A moment later she appeared in the passage, her hands clasped in front of her, her black eyes remote, her face dead pan.

178

I moved back, waving her into my room. She walked in and I shut the door.

She was the original ice woman. Moving to a chair, she sat down, crossed her legs and rested her hands in her lap. Her black, glittering eyes regarded me.

I went over to another chair away from her and sat down, holding the Mauser so she could see it.

" Quit stalling, Beth . . . is it yes or no?"

Her cold remoteness fazed me.

" I have something to say first," she said.

" You have? Okay, then make it short. What do you want to say?"

I wanted to put pressure on her, but I could see she was determined to take her time. She leaned back, completely relaxed, then she smiled at me: that hateful, jeering little smile I had come to know.

" I want to thank you for doing me the greatest favour anyone could have done for me."

I stiffened, staring at her.

" Favour? What do you mean?"

" I'll tell you. For years sex and men were the only things I could think about. To me, men were my food and drink. When Ross turned up, ruthless, young, marvellous in bed, I became utterly besotted with him. He was my ideal man: tough, ruthless and utterly wonderful, sexually. My life revolved around him. I could think of nothing else but him. When he wasn't with me, I burned for him."

I moved uneasily.

" Do I have to listen to your erotic talk? I'm not interested. I . . ."

" You had better listen!" The snap in her voice cut me short. " He was ambitious. He longed for money. I married Frank, knowing he would be rich, only to please Ross. I told myself I would do anything so he could have the money, even letting a creep like you make love to me . . . even murder because I believed Ross was a real man." She lifted her hands in a gesture of despair, then let them drop to her lap. " What is a real man? Not you. You with all your talk about being an expert with money! Frank, drunk as he was, knew so much better than you did. I could have had three million instead of one million if you had let him alone to do that steel deal, but you thought you were so smart. Then you turned black-mailer. A real man? Ask yourself. How do you think you add up?"

" Never mind the talk, Beth. That's all water under the bridge," I said, hating her. " Anyone can make a mistake . . ."

She went on as if she hadn't heard me. " For four years, I idolised Ross and now what do I find I have been idolising?" She leaned forward, her black eyes glittering and spat out the words: " A cringing, gutless, cowering coward! A yellow creep who is so frightened he is impotent! A louse who cringes in a dark room because he is afraid of you . . . that's what I find I have got!" She drew in a deep breath, then went on, " So that's why I am thanking you for a big favour. You have shown me the kind of gutless louse I thought I loved. Well, thanks to you, I love him no more. I now hate the sight of him. Go ahead and shoot him. That's all he deserves. You are not getting one cent from me! Go ahead and shoot him. I'll be glad to be rid of him!"

I stared at her. Looking at her hard dead pan face, I felt a sudden uneasiness. I told myself she was bluffing. She had to be bluffing!

" You don't fool me!" I shouted at her. " I'll kill him! That's for real, but I'll give you one more chance. Now come on . . . you know you are bluffing and I don't bluff."

She got up and walked to the door.

" Wait, Beth!"

She paused and looked at me. Her contemptuous little smile was like a knife thrust.

" I'm going to have that money!" I yelled at her. " You either pay up or Ross gets shot!"

She nodded.

" I would like that. Do me a favour . . . kill him," and leaving the room, she walked down the passage.

I jumped up and ran to the door.

" Beth !"

She didn't pause. She opened the front door and walked out into the sunshine and back to *Apple Trees.*

*　　*　　*

Was she bluffing?

I sat at the window, staring at *Apple Trees.* I watched her walk into the bungalow and shut the door. The red curtains were still drawn. Was Ross cringing in the darkened room or was he waiting for her, a grin on his face while she told him of her bluff?

I fingered the Mauser.

Then I suddenly realised, if she wasn't bluffing, if she really had had enough of Ross, I would have to think twice about going out there and shooting him.

I had got away with Marshall's murder, but shooting Ross was something I couldn't hide up. Beth would call the police and give them some story that I was blackmailing her and Ross had tried to protect her and I had shot him. With Bernstein and her money behind her, I wouldn't stand a prayer.

My bluff had looked good to me, but she had called it. So long as she was infatuated with Ross, my threat stood up, but Ross, turning coward, had fixed me. With sick frustration, I knew now I wouldn't kill him.

I could think of no other way to get the money from her. Once again I had the sickening feeling that no matter what I did to lay my hands on big money, I always fluffed it.

I had to admit it. Beth had beaten me. There was now no reason for me to stay in this little house. I would pack and get out. I thought of my life ahead : grabbing at any damn job for eating money. Then I remembered Bert and his offer to make me his partner. Why not? I remembered what Sheriff McQueen had said : *Why not stay on at Wicksteed? Bert still wants you to be his partner*. Why not? I thought of Wicksteed and Mrs. Hansen and Maisie and the rest of them : a nice little town and nice people. Why not? I could settle there. Maybe later, I could get married. Suddenly, I didn't give a damn about Marshall's million nor Beth nor Ross. I would go back to Wicksteed. I would help Bert set up a U-drive service. I'd organise a Travel agency for him. In a couple of years, I could be as prosperous as Joe Pinner!

Getting to my feet, I felt a surge of confidence. Okay, I would never be in the real money class, but at least, I could be a success in Wicksteed and what was the matter with that? Let Beth and Ross go to hell together. If she didn't want him, if she hadn't been bluffing, let her go off on her own. Why should I care?

I looked at the Mauser in my hand. It now seemed incredible to me that I had bought the gun and that I really meant to kill Ross. I must have been out of my mind. I must get rid of the gun as soon as I could . . . throw it in a ditch or somewhere.

I now had an urgent need to get away. Then I thought of Mrs. Brody. I couldn't just walk out without giving her some explanation. After a moment's thought, I decided I would tell her my wife had been taken ill. That would do. I would leave her a note.

Taking my suitcase from the closet, I packed. In ten minutes I was ready to go.

I wrote a brief note to Mrs. Brody and I enclosed two weeks rent. I wrote that as soon as my wife recovered, I would get in touch with her.

Shoving the Mauser in my hip-pocket, picking up the suitcase and the typewriter, I started down the passage, then as I reached the living-room, I paused.

I couldn't remember ever feeling so relaxed and confident. The thought that in a few hours I would be in Bert's office, drinking a shot of whisky, talking about our future plans was like a shot in the arm.

I thought of Ross, probably still hiding behind the red curtains. I felt suddenly magnanimous. I put down the type-writer and suitcase. Why not? Why not call Beth and tell her she had won? What was the matter with that? Why not wish her luck with the money that was coming to her? Why not show her I was, after all, a real man?

I went into the living-room and dialled Beth's number. As I waited, I heard myself humming under my breath. In a few minutes I would be rid of them both and driving to Wick-steed. I could imagine Mrs. Hansen's pleased expression when she saw me and Bert's delighted grin.

Then I heard a click and Ross said, " Who is it?"

" Devery," I said. " I want to speak to Beth."

A long pause, then Ross said, " You're too late. I've fixed her and I've fixed you," and he gave a hysterical giggle that sent a surge of cold blood up my spine.

" What are you talking about?"

" You made me do it! There was only one way out for me. I wanted to call the cops, but she wouldn't let me! So as she couldn't fix you, I've fixed her! I would rather spend fourteen years in a cell than walk into a bullet! I've called the police. They'll protect me from you. They are on their way now."

The cold dead finger crept up my spine.

" Ross! What are you saying?" I shouted.

He giggled again. He sounded slightly out of his head.

" I worked it out. If she didn't get the money, you wouldn't shoot me. She came back and told me to get out. She said she had had enough of me. She said she would be glad if you shot me! She wouldn't let me near the telephone. I wanted to call the police, so I fixed her. I hit her with an axe. Her brains are all over the goddamn room." He caught his breath in a sob. " The police are coming. I warned you . . . you made me kill her . . . I've had enough."

I dropped the receiver on its cradle.

His voice, the hysterical giggles, the sob told me this wasn't bluff.

My world began to fall to pieces. Even as I stood there, cold sweat running down my face, I heard the sound of a distant siren.

I had to get out!

I snatched up my suitcase and typewriter, ran down the path and got in my car. As I started the engine, a police car swept by.

As I drove down to the highway, panic gripped me. Ross would talk. He would tell the police the whole story, then they would come after me. Reaching the bottom of the road, I waited for the lights to change. Where would I go? Not to Wicksteed. I would head north.

The lights changed, but I didn't drive forward. My brain was beginning to function : panic was subsiding.

Marshall's murder was foolproof. I was sure of that. No matter what Ross said, the police wouldn't be able to pin a murder rap on me. If I could keep my nerve, stand up to their questions, I could still get away with it, but not if I ran away.

As I was thinking, an ambulance stormed by me, heading for *Apple Trees*. Then two more police cars went by. Again panic nibbled at my mind.

I thought of Wicksteed. If I could beat the rap, I could go back there. It was a gamble. It would be tough going with my jail record, but what had I to lose? I could get away with it. It would be Ross's word against mine. Maybe the police would be convinced I had killed Marshall, but they couldn't prove it. It would depend on the jury. Everyone in Wicksteed liked me and they hated Beth. They wouldn't believe I had murdered Marshall. They would put all the blame on Beth and Ross.

Rather than run, I decided, I would gamble. I shifted into reverse and drove slowly back up the road towards Mrs. Brody's house.

Then I remembered the Mauser. The gun would be a complete give away. It would support Ross's story.

Pulling up, I took the gun from my hip-pocket. It wouldn't take the police long to find the pawnbroker who had sold it to me and from him they would get my description. I remembered his long, thoughtful stare as he sold me the gun. He would remember me all right. The police then would have a foot in the door and they would crowd around me, shouting questions, want to know why I had bought the gun if Ross was lying, why I was staying with Mrs. Brody under the name of Lucas. They would keep on and on and sooner or later, they would break me. I couldn't face that. I looked at the Mauser. I would keep it with me. It offered a quick way out, but first, I would give them a run.

I turned into a lay-by, backed the car and headed back to the highway.

The sun was shining and the sky was blue as I headed north. I thought of the five years of hell I had spent in jail. I wasn't going to spend another fourteen years locked in a cell. I patted the Mauser: a quick way out.

As I drove I thought of Frank Marshall. Drunk though he had been, he wasn't a bad guy. I thought of Wicksteed and all the nice people who lived there, but I had no thoughts of Beth.

Before long, the police would catch up with me, but I still had some money and my freedom for a few more days.

As I trode down on the gas pedal, I touched the Mauser again.

www.ingramcontent.com/pod-product-compliance
Ingram Content Group UK Ltd.
Pitfield, Milton Keynes, MK11 3LW, UK
UKHW022311280225
455674UK00004B/262